KASSY O'ROARKE

CUB REPORTER

D0062067

KASSY O'ROARKE

CUB REPORTER

PET DETECTIVE MYSTERIES
BOOK ONE

KELLY OLIVER

—Beaver's Pond Press—
Minneapolis, MN

PRAISE FOR *KASSY O'ROARKE, CUB REPORTER*

"A juicy middle-grade mystery in which a young investigator learns that it's okay to be vulnerable."

—*Foreword Reviews*

"A polished, convincing, kid-centered adventure, with endearing characters and a strong sense of middle-school humor. Oliver writes in a breezy, kid-friendly style that's perfect for early middle schoolers, who will easily identity with Kassy. A strong series debut!"

—*BlueInk Review*

"An action-packed and exciting adventure mystery novel. *Kassy O'Roarke, Cub Reporter* is well-written and likely to entertain both animal and mystery lovers of all ages. It's most highly recommended!"

—Jeff Mangus, *Readers' Favorite*

"A whole lot of fun—and delivers in every way an adventure story should! The mystery's twists and turns are clever and unpredictable, but Kelly Oliver builds more than a detailed mystery. She also creates a heartwarming world populated with believable characters who feel like people you know."

—Sarah Scheele, *Readers' Favorite*

"Great fun, with its underpants-wearing animals and many memorable characters, like Flatulent Freddie the farting ferret. The book is action-packed, and the characters are all likable and realistic, with relatable problems. The plot has twists and turns that are sure to keep readers on their toes. I was hooked by the first page!"

—Kristen Van Campen (teen reviewer), *Readers' Favorite*

"This is a purely enjoyable adventure filled with memorable characters, an endearing protagonist, and a lot of heart."

—US Review of Books

"For everyone who's into adventure, mystery, and a whole bunch of middle-grade fun, this first in series does the trick! Beware, you won't want to set this book down anytime soon."

—Chanticleer Reviews

Proofread by Paige Polinsky

Illustrated by BNP Design Studio

Production editor: Hanna Kjeldbjerg

Cover illustration by BNP Design Studio

ISBN 13: 978 1-64343-903-7

Library of Congress Catalog Number: 2019913329

Printed in the United States of America

First Printing: 2020

24 23 22 21 20   5 4 3 2 1

Book design by Athena Currier

Beaver's Pond Press
7108 Ohms Lane
Edina, MN 55439–2129

(952) 829-8818

www.BeaversPondPress.com

To order, visit www.ItascaBooks.com
or call (800) 901-3480 ext. 118. Reseller discounts available.

For media inquiries, please call or e-mail Kelly Oliver at kellyoliverbooks@gmail.com.
For more information, visit www.kellyoliverbooks.com.

This book is dedicated to cat lovers, big and small.

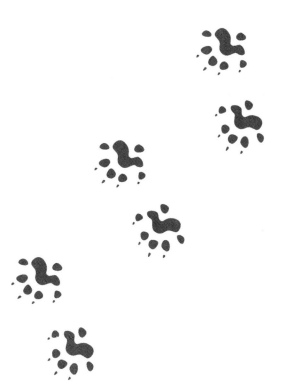

1

LOOKING FOR A SCOOP

THE LAST BELL RINGS. I rush out of class, dash down the hall, and skid to a stop in front of the newspaper rack. I grab the new issue of the school paper. The *Cub Reporter* is hot off the press. My palms are damp, and I'm panting just a little bit. Knowing my article is somewhere in these pages makes my skin tingle all over. I squeeze through the crowded hallway and pop out the front door of the school building. I want to be alone when I see my name in print for the first time.

The air outside is cool, but the sun warms my face. I head for my favorite spot, under the ginkgo tree. It's my secret place to sit and spy on the other kids. Around the tree, daffodils are in full bloom. The ginkgo's leaves look like tiny green fans

1

waving from its branches. I plop down on the grass, glance around, and then dig into the paper.

I push my glasses back on my nose and flip through the pages. *Where's my article?* I scan the paper again, but it's not there. I go back through page by stinking page. My heart sinks. Maybe they didn't publish it after all. *Wait. What?* I stare down at the very last page. *Brussels sprouts!* There it is. My story's in a tiny corner on the last page, where no one will ever read it. I guess no one cares about changes to the school lunch program.

So, who got the lead story? I turn the paper over. There's her name in bold print, my nemesis, Kelly Finkelman, one of the most popular girls in school. I'd rather eat her article than read it, but I force myself to pass my eyes over the words. What's so great about Smelly Kelly and her story on—*whoa.*

A police car pulls into the parking lot. *What's going on?* Did

a teacher have a heart attack? Or maybe a kid got caught stealing? Or, worse, was someone kidnapped? My mind is racing.

A uniformed officer gets out of the car and heads toward the school entrance. I jump up to follow him. Mrs. Cheever says a good reporter has a nose for crime and goes after the scoop. And I need a scoop if I'm going to get my next story on the front page of the newspaper.

The police officer turns around. *Holy hot on his heels!* I'm so close I nearly crash into him.

"Excuse me, miss," he says, smiling down at me. "Do you know where I might find Kelly Finkelman?"

"The cheerleader?" I ask, then realize how stupid I sound. "Is she in trouble?" I can't imagine Miss Goody-Two-Shoes getting in trouble.

"No." The police officer laughs. "I'm here to thank her. Without her story, we wouldn't have caught the vandal this morning."

"Vandal?" I ask. "What vandal?"

"The man who spray-painted yellow curses all over the school's brand-new Astroturf."

"Oh." I nod. That explains why a cleaning team is scrubbing the fake grass behind the school. I point toward the other end of the school building. "Kelly's probably in the gym at cheer practice."

"Thanks," the officer says and then heads inside the double glass doors.

I slink back to my spot under the gingko tree. I snap the head off a daffodil and sniff it. The sour smell makes me sneeze. I wipe pollen off my nose, and my fingers turn yellow. *Wait a second!* I glimpsed him, the spray paint guy. The dude was wearing a hoodie and carrying a can. *Fried dill pickles!* It had to be him. I could kick myself. If only I'd gone to investigate . . .

"That could've been my story," I say under my breath. Chirping makes me look up. On a branch overhead, a bright red cardinal sings in agreement, "You, you, you, you, you, dim-wit, wit, wit, wit."

Were it not for my little brother, I could've caught the vandal. Then the police officer would be congratulating me instead of Smelly Kelly with her perfect Barbie doll hair.

Speak of the deviled egg, Miss Front-Page News is coming through the door. Kelly is all smiles as she follows the officer to his patrol car. He pulls out something from the front seat. It's a gold medal hanging on a purple ribbon. He puts it around Kelly's perfect neck. She's beaming as he shakes her hand. "Good work, young lady," the officer says. "Well done."

I have to admit, that's a pretty cool medal. I tear a velvety petal off the flower and roll it between my thumb and fingers until it's a sticky ball, then flick it toward the police car. *Yuck.* Now my fingers are sticky. I rub my tacky fingers back and forth on my jeans to get the gluey petal juice off.

I wave at Kelly as she skips up the sidewalk on her way back inside the building. She doesn't even see me. It's like I'm invisible. You know what's weird? Sometimes everyone is staring at me, and other times no one sees me at all, like I don't even exist. Why do people only notice me when I'm doing something stupid?

That's all going to change when I get my scoop, a really big scoop, a front-page-story kind of scoop . . . something that will make everyone—even Smelly Kelly—stop and say, "Kassy O'Roarke, *Cub* reporter, is going places."

I'm going to write the best story of the year, get a prime spot on the newspaper, and win the Thompson Award for Journalism. My middle school gives it out each spring for the best article in the school newspaper that year. It's named after Jerry Thompson, a local reporter who was nominated for a Pulitzer Prize, which is a huge deal in journalism. If I win, everyone will know I exist—and not because I'm doing something stupid or weird but because I'm doing something good. By everyone, I don't just mean Smelly Kelly and the other kids but also Mom and Dad . . . especially Dad.

Dad thinks I go around with my head in the clouds. "Earth to Kassy" is his favorite thing to say. I'll show him I can *do* something, something really important, like catch thieves and stop criminals. I'll prove I can do something besides daydream. Then maybe he'll finally come back home.

"Hi, Kassy." The familiar voice from behind the bushes almost gives me a heart attack.

When I jump up, a tree branch whacks me in the face and knocks my glasses off. "You scared the cookies out of me!" I snatch my glasses up out of the dirt and blow on them. "Don't sneak up on me like that, Crispy."

Crispy is my little brother. His real name is Perseus, but everyone else calls him Percy. He's named after a Greek superhero who can fly. As far as I know, Percy's only superpower is putting his shirt on backward and snorting milk out of his nose. I call him *Crispy* on account of the time he accidently burned down our hay barn trying to keep Luke and Leia warm. Luke and Leia are our goats. They were babies back then.

When it happened, Mom didn't even yell. All she said was, "I'm just glad no one got hurt."

But that's not true. Everyone got hurt. The fire was the straw that broke the camel's back (don't worry—our camel, Spittoon, still has his hump in just the right place). The week after the fire, Dad took off for downtown Nashville, and then animals started talking to Crispy.

I brush grass off my butt and glare at my little brother. "What are you doing here? You were supposed to wait for me at school." Crispy's elementary school is only three blocks from mine, but Mom still insists I go pick him up and walk him home. She also makes me hold his hand. It's embarrassing.

"I wanna get home to my cake." Crispy's red hair is sticking out in all directions. His face is red, and he's squinting at me with his green cat eyes.

Freddie the ferret's pointy nose peeks out of my brother's backpack. The ferret's black mask makes him look like a furry bandit. I call him *Flatulent Freddie* because, well, he farts a lot.

Technically, Crispy isn't supposed to take the animals off our property, but he just isn't himself without a furry friend. Sometimes I wonder if my little brother is really a rodent disguised as a human.

"What are you doing?" Crispy asks, taking Freddie out of his pack and snuggling him. "Is that a new notebook?"

"None of your wax." I flip the notebook shut. Crispy is always following me around. He can be such a pest.

When Freddie sits up on Crispy's shoulder, I notice the keys in his paws. "Whose keys are those?" I ask.

"Freddie!" Crispy takes the keys away from the ferret. "Oh no! He stole Mrs. Smith's keys again."

I grab my backpack from under the tree. "We'd better walk back to your school and return them before you and Freddie get in trouble."

Crispy doesn't mean to get in trouble. His nearly-eight-year-old brain just doesn't think things through. Not like me. Dad says I spend too much time thinking instead of just being a kid—whatever that means. But I won't always be a kid. Someday I'll be a detective or a spy. Anyway, if I'm going to write a killer story and win the Thompson Award, I'll have to use my brain.

"Are you writing a riddle?" Crispy asks.

"No, I'm writing an article for the school newspaper."

"Wow. Really?" Crispy slides the ferret into his sweater. "What's it about?"

I wave my notebook back and forth to diffuse Freddie's musky smell. It's a cool notebook. I saved up my allowance and bought it at a fancy notebook store. The emerald-green cover flips open like a real detective notebook. I love the way the plastic feels cool and smooth against my fingers. Mom got me a pint-size pen to go with it. I slide my notebook into a pocket of my spy vest. It's really one of Dad's old fishing vests with tons of pockets to carry my spy stuff.

"I'm waiting for my big break," I answer. "Come on, let's go."

Crispy holds out his hand, and I force myself to take it. It's sticky and hot, but I hold on to it anyway.

"A break? Won't that hurt?" Crispy looks up at me like a puppy waiting for a treat.

I close my eyes and exhale out loud. "A *break* as in a big story. I need something to happen so I can write about it." I pull at Crispy's arm to make him walk faster.

"Like what?" When he stumbles, I slow down and wait for him.

"Murder, mischief, mayhem," I say.

Crispy stops suddenly, jerking my arm half out of its socket. He stands there blinking up at me like a hamster. "You mean that scoop thing you're always talking about?"

"Exactly. I'm a keen observer, and I have the courage to follow my story all the way to the truth," I say, repeating Mrs. Cheever's words. She's my English teacher and the newspaper advisor.

Crispy gapes at me.

"I'm waiting for someone to commit a crime or something so I can report it." I pull on his arm.

"You wish someone would commit a crime?"

"Well, maybe not murder or anything violent." I shake my head. "Maybe burglary or larceny or cheating at cards?" It comes out as a question.

"What's larceny?"

"Thieving, stealing, pilfering, robbing, nicking." Can you tell I read the dictionary every night before bed? I'm actually only up to the letter *H*. Mrs. Cheever says that to be a good journalist, I have to work on my vocabulary.

"What do you want them to steal?" Crispy asks. His face lights up as if he likes the idea. And I thought Freddie was the only klepto in the family.

I yank on Crispy's arm again to get him going. "They could start by taking you and Freddie."

"That's not stealing. It's kidnapping."

"Okay, smarty-pants. Just Freddie. Ferret-napping."

Crispy bows his head and whispers into his sweater, "Don't worry. I'll protect you." Freddie squeaks in response.

"Come on, slowpoke. Get a move on or we'll be late for your birthday party. I'm sure all your furry friends are waiting for a piece of cake."

"That's why I asked for carrot cake. So I could share." Crispy kisses the ferret on his little black nose.

"Very thoughtful of you." I don't bother telling him vegetables don't belong in dessert.

"Apollo says it's not what we have but what we share that matters." Crispy smiles and pecks Freddie on the nose again.

"Apollo told you that?" I drop his hand. Sometimes my brother astounds me. But this takes the carrot cake. Mom tells me to humor him because he's "so smart and sensitive." *Whatever!*

I want to tell my brother he's a few slices short of a birthday cake, but I just say, "I guess Apollo is pretty smart for a cougar cub."

2
THE BIRTHDAY PARTY

UNDERPANTS! AFTER DOING MY homework and reading a few more pages of the dictionary, I come out to the barn for Crispy's birthday party, and what do I see? All the animals are wearing underpants. They're going nuts. The petting zoo is a circus of whinnies, screeches, grunts, and snorts. *Why are they all wearing underpants?*

Spittoon the camel has on some giant droopy drawers. Athena the anteater is sporting Mom's silky pink panties. Raider the raccoon is wearing—*wait, are those Dad's briefs? Where did those come from?* Dad hasn't been here for over a year. *What the—?* Kylo Ren the rooster is wearing one of my American Girl dolls' underpants wrapped around his tail feathers. Poseidon the piglet is running around in my Hello Kitty undies. *Ha-ha. Very funny.*

I capture Poseidon and wrestle him out of my underwear. Hello Kitty has a hoof-sized hole in her face where her mouth would be if she had one. My favorite underpants are ruined. "Percy 'Crispy' O'Roarke, where are you? I'm going to throttle you!" Now I know where Crispy disappeared to after school. *Now I know.* He was dressing the animals again.

Crispy comes around the corner of the barn carrying a stack of birthday hats. The animals get excited and start making even more noise. I cover my ears until they calm down. They love Crispy, and he loves them. He says they're his only friends, which is sweet but also kind of sad.

After Dad moved out, Crispy didn't speak for months. He didn't say a word until Mom opened the petting zoo. Then he started talking to the rescue animals. You wouldn't believe all the wild animals and strange creatures people bring to Mom's vet clinic. That's how she started the petting zoo, with rescue animals. We have Morpheus, the pony rescued from a breeder; Spittoon, the camel rescued from a circus; Chewbacca, the chimp rescued from a lab; Raider, the raccoon rescued as an abandoned baby; Apollo, the cougar cub rescued from a hunter; and then some regular farm animals, like Poseidon the pig and Kylo Ren the rooster.

Crispy snaps a colorful cone onto Chewbacca's round head and tightens the elastic band around her chin. Flatulent Freddie is riding on Crispy's shoulder. Why is Freddie the only one without undies? Better yet, why is everyone else wearing them?

"What's with the underpants?" I ask.

"I don't want anybody to have an accident during my birthday party."

I narrow my eyes at my brother. "Ah, shouldn't you put them in diapers? I doubt flimsy underpants can contain the output of most of these super-duper poopers." The smells emanating from our petting zoo are legendary. A dozen species from across the animal kingdom put off some warm, spicy odors. Once you get used to it, the smell's kind of comforting. It wraps itself around you like a warm blanket on a cold day. It becomes the smell of home.

"Only babies wear diapers," Crispy says. "We're not babies, are we, Freddie?"

I do a double take. I swear that ferret nodded.

"Well, Apollo's a baby." I look around for the cougar cub. His pen is empty. I glance around the barn to check if he's in another enclosure, but the new barn is so big I can't see all the pens at once. It's the kind of barn you might see at a fairground, more like a huge warehouse with a dirt floor and a gigantic roof on top of wooden rafters. The high ceiling of the barn amplifies the sounds of cawing, snorting, and whinnying. I raise my voice to be heard over the ruckus. "Did you take Apollo to watch cartoons again?"

"We watch *animated shorts*, not *cartoons*."

"Whatever you say, Crispy. So, where is he?"

Crispy shrugs. He isn't supposed to take the animals out of their pens. He's gotten in trouble more than once for carrying the little cougar cub upstairs to his bedroom. Apollo is actually a three-month-old cougar cub. Mom says baby *Puma concolor* are called *kittens* and not *cubs*. She says even though Apollo's cute and cuddly, he's a wild animal and shouldn't be in the house.

Speak of the deviled egg, Mom appears at the door carrying a cake and a carton of milk. She's wearing overalls, boots, and a flannel shirt. With her pixie haircut, she looks like a miniature lumberjack. All smiles, she balances the cake and milk on top of a sawhorse and then pulls wooden matches out of her overalls. I wince and glance at Crispy, thinking about how much damage one little match can do.

"Happy birthday, Skunk," Mom says. Crispy hates it when she calls him *Skunk*. I think it's hilarious.

Mom starts singing "Happy Birthday." She nods at me to join in.

What choice do I have? I sing along, then add, "Happy birthday to you. You were born in a zoo. You look like a monkey, and you smell like one too." With his cowlick sticking straight up, Crispy looks more like an orangutan that put its finger in a light socket.

"Make a wish and blow out your candles." Mom holds up a plastic spatula. "Then you can cut the cake and share with our furry friends."

Crispy takes a deep breath, leans forward, and blows until his cheeks turn red. He blows out all eight candles. In his excitement, he accidently kicks the sawhorse, and his cake topples into the sawdust. The milk carton lands upright in the middle of the mess.

"Oh no!" Crispy's smile turns into a frown.

Nothing like sawdust sprinkles to spice up a gluten-free birthday cake full of orange vegetables. *Hey, maybe now we won't have to eat it!*

"Sawdust, carrots . . . what's the difference?" I say under my breath. Knowing Mom, the cake is not only gluten-free, but also sugar-free, dairy-free, and thus taste-free. When referring to anything Mom bakes, *cake* is just a figure of speech. *Dog biscuit* is more like it.

Mom scowls. "Oh no. Poor little Skunk." She ruffles Crispy's hair. "I think we can salvage enough to each have a taste."

I bend down to scrape the "cake" out of the dirt. I pull the milk carton out of the mess. Holding it by the handle, I lick cream cheese frosting off its plastic sides.

"Leave it be," Mom says. She pulls out forks from her overalls and passes them around. "Best we eat the top layer rather than risk moving it and contaminating the rest." She plops down in the dust next to the cake. Crispy does the same. It takes more than a dusty cake to get Mom upset. She's unflappable, which means it takes a lot to get her to flap.

Oh well, what's more chicken poop on my favorite corduroy skirt? I knew I shouldn't have dressed up for a party in the petting zoo. I sit down and dig into the cake. I have to admit, it's pretty tasty once you pick off the sawdust.

Mom pours us each a glass of milk and raises hers. "A toast to the Three Musketeers." She laughs. Mom's laugh is contagious, and I start laughing too.

"Mouseketeers," I say.

Crispy laughs so hard milk comes out his nose. I told you that's his superpower.

Chewy is making a ruckus, banging her aluminum plate against the wall. "*Hoooooo. Oooo. Oooo,*" she whoops, jumping up and down.

Crispy lets the chimp out of her enclosure. She runs to the pile of cake, grabs big globs, and stuffs them into her mouth—well, more like *onto* her mouth. Her furry chin is covered with a white frosting beard. Chimps love carrot cake. Most of the animals in our petting zoo love Mom's cooking. Maybe because what she bakes is not fit for human consumption.

"Save some for Spittoon and Raider," Crispy says as he grabs the chimp's arm and pulls her onto his lap. She leans in for another helping. My brother slides her off his lap, scoops up a handful of cake, stands up, then walks over and deposits it into the camel's trough. Spittoon ambles over, sniffs, and shakes his head. He's not impressed.

I chuckle to myself. I know how he feels.

After Raider washes his paws in his water bowl, he helps himself to the sawdust-covered remains. The raccoon gobbles handfuls of cake, making smacking noises and hardly coming up for air.

"We all need to learn a lesson from Raider," Mom says. "Raccoons always wash their hands before dinner."

"But he eats like a pig," I say, and then I turn to our piglet. "No offense, Poseidon."

"Delicious cake," Crispy says with his mouth full. Like all the other farm animals, he loves Mom's weird recipes. Then again, my little brother eats beetles and dandelions too.

Sometimes he joins Spittoon, Luke, Leia, and Morpheus when they graze in the pasture. Crispy crawls around on all fours, munching on grass just like the other herbivores. No wonder he likes vegetables in his desserts.

Mom gasps. "Oh, my. Why is Raider wearing your dad's underpants?" A mouthful of cake makes her giggle sound like a snort. Her dark eyes twinkle mischievously as she covers her smile with her hand. "Who wore them better?" she asks, eyes glistening.

Holy hysteria. Mom's gone off the deep end. "Are you okay?" I pat her on the back.

Still smiling, she nods and wipes her eyes with the back of her hands. She stands up and brushes off her overalls. "Let's make sure all the animals have their dinners. Skunk, you fill their water bowls while I measure out their meals. Petunia, make sure everyone else who wants cake gets some."

Aargh. I wish she wouldn't call me *Petunia.* Why do parents always have to pick such embarrassing nicknames? Being named after the ancient Greek prophet Kassandra is bad enough. Hopefully my nickname came from the flower and not from Petunia Pig, Mom's favorite cartoon character.

"Where's Apollo?" Mom's face turns the color of cream cheese frosting. "Percy, did you take Apollo to your room again? Honey, he's safer staying in his pen."

Crispy looks up from Spittoon's water trough. "No. He's not in my room."

"Kassy, did you leave his enclosure open?"

"I didn't touch his enclosure." How can Mom even think I would do something so irresponsible? I glower at Crispy. He's always getting me into trouble.

"Drop what you're doing. We've got to find him." Mom wipes her hands on her overalls and runs toward the house. "If we don't find Apollo," she shouts, "I'll have to call Animal Control and report him missing!" She quickly opens the outside gate, closes it behind her, and calls back over her shoulder, "A cougar kitten on the loose. This could cost us the farm!"

My stomach seizes up into a tight knot. It's true. Mr. and Mrs. Busybody have already complained to Animal Control once—after Spittoon escaped, trampled their flower bed, and ate the leaves off their hydrangea bushes. Animal Control agent Pinkerton Killjoy is just waiting for another breakout to close us down. I guess Mom is right. In the eyes of Animal Control, a vegetarian camel is one thing; a carnivorous lion is quite another.

"You're not hiding Apollo in your room, are you?" I glare at Crispy.

"No, he's not in my room."

"Cross your heart and hope to die?" I make a cross over my chest, and then Crispy does the same.

"Pinkie swear?" I hold out my pinkie, and Crispy hooks his smaller pinkie around mine.

"I swear," he says. "Apollo is not in my bedroom."

An itchy feeling in the corner of my eyes warns me I'm about to start crying. *Detectives, spies, and reporters don't cry,* I remind myself, sniffling. But what if Mom is right and we lose everything? My heart is galloping faster than our pony after he eats all the apples off the apple tree.

"Don't worry. We'll find Apollo." Crispy looks up at me, grinning like a baboon. "Now you've got your scoop. What's bigger than a missing lion?"

"He's just a cub." I wipe my eyes on my sleeve. "Aren't you worried?"

"I know you'll find him because you're a great detective."

I try to talk, but I can't. No words will come out. I can barely breathe. In the dictionary, I read about hyperventilating. It's like panting, only it's for humans. That must be what's happening to me. I squat down and put my face in my hands. My hands feel clammy against my cheeks. Even my fingers are shaking.

Crispy's right. It's up to me. I've got to find Apollo and save the petting zoo. Our whole future is in my trembling hands.

3
GATHERING CLUES

BY SUNDOWN, A GLOOMY PALL has spread over the petting zoo. Even the animals sense our future is at stake. Usually, dinnertime is a celebration and the animals hoot, holler, and dance to the rhythms of their happy bellies. This evening, they wait in silence.

Mom is out searching the woods. I haven't seen her this upset since Dad left. I grit my teeth, remembering when she spent a whole week in bed. I brought her tea and crackers and stood in her bedroom doorway watching her cry her heart out. It was like she'd folded in on herself and the rest of the world had disappeared. "Please, please, please, bring her back to me," I begged. Then I tiptoed to her bedside to take her hand. "I love you, Mom," I whispered. But she just stared at me with her eyes glazed over. I can't let that happen to her again. I won't let it happen. It's up to me to find Apollo and save the petting zoo.

Stomach acid burns a hole in my gut, and I want to barf. The tiny cub can't survive on his own. My eyes are burning. I hold my breath and dig my fingernails into the palm of my hand. If I start crying again, I'll drown in my own tears. I've just got to find Apollo or he'll die. And if Animal Control finds out he's missing, it'll close us down. Then we'll lose everything. I've got to find him, I've just got to. I ball my hands into fists and pace the length of the barn. *Concentrate! Use your Vulcan brain!* I've got to calm down and think this through.

Okay. I run through the possibilities in my mind. *Someone kidnapped him.* That would be the worst. *Or maybe Crispy took him to his room again and he's just hiding in a closet. Or maybe Crispy left the gate open and he wandered off. The cub might have snuck out of his pen and joined one of his buddies.* I just need to search all the pens again . . . then I'll find him.

Each animal has its own large enclosure. Some animals, like the camel and pony, need only a wooden fence. But others—the ones who can jump or climb, like the cub and chimp—need chicken wire all around their pens. They all have their own houses inside and outside so if it rains on the weekend—the only time we're open to the public—we don't have to close the petting zoo.

I go back and search every pen, stall, and enclosure inside the barn and out. Over and over again, I search, but Apollo is nowhere to be found.

I double-check Spittoon's pen. Apollo and Spittoon are fast friends, which is funny since Spittoon is allergic to cats. Have you ever seen a camel sneeze? It's not pretty. Now, missing his mountain lion friend, the camel just hangs his head and won't touch his dinner.

After checking inside the house, including every inch of Crispy's bedroom, I make yet another trip around the outside of the barn. I inspect every pen and enclosure inside, and then give up my search. I drop down next to Crispy on a bench near Apollo's empty pen. I don't know what to do next. I've searched everywhere. I prop my elbows on my knees and put my chin in my hands.

"Why aren't you looking for Apollo?" I ask. "Aren't you scared?"

"I've been interviewing the witnesses." Crispy smiles over at me. "Spittoon knows where he is."

Yeah, right. I'm too tired to argue. Distractedly, I watch the animals eat their dinners, hoping Apollo will wander in from his hiding place. Chewy chomps a banana, wearing the peel on her head while she eats the fruit. Morpheus munches on a pile of hay. Yoda the tortoise carries a lettuce leaf in his mouth, and when his head retracts into his shell, he looks like an exotic plant. Darth Vader is on his perch watching over us like a hawk (which he is).

Can you tell which animals Mom named and which ones Crispy named? Mom says, "The ancient Greeks had Mount Olympus, and we have *Star Wars.*"

Usually, Darth Vader has to guard his bowl of raw meat or Apollo will eat it. But tonight the hawk doesn't have to worry. I brush away another tear with the back of my hand. Luckily, I always keep tissues in a pocket of my spy vest. I take one out and blow my nose.

Mom rushes into the barn and throws her hands into the air. *Deep-fried okra!* Her eyes are red and swollen like she's been crying. "I've looked everywhere." She plops down on the bench next to me. "Where can he be?" She buries her head in her hands. I hand her a tissue.

My face is on fire, and the corner of my eyes are itchy again. I don't know what to do. I've just got to save Apollo or Mom might have another nervous breakdown. That's what Grandma called it when Mom couldn't get out of bed for a week after Dad left. A *nervous breakdown.* I shut my eyes and take a deep breath. I've already lost Dad. I don't want to lose Mom again too.

Crispy's right. I've got to put on my detective thinking cap and solve the case. Mind racing, I get up and pace the length of the barn again, scanning every enclosure, pen, and cage as I go. Wiping my cheeks on my sleeve, I try not to let Mom see I'm crying. I count the animals, making sure no one else is missing. Eleven other animals are where they should be, but no sign of Apollo.

I slide the big barn door open and look outside again. The chain-link fence around the barn seems secure, and the gate is closed. I take a quick tour of the outside enclosures just in case, but they're all empty. I go back inside the barn, sit down next to Mom, and take her hand. Her hand is trembling. I let go. I can hardly breathe. I might barf. I inhale the scent of damp fur, hay, and sawdust. The smell calms me down.

"Focus," I tell myself. *Spies, detectives, and journalists don't hyperventilate, barf, or cry. Instead, they look for clues and use their brains to solve the case.* And that's just what I'm going to do. I'm going to put on my detective thinking cap and use my brain to figure out what happened to Apollo.

"Let's review the facts," I say, pulling myself together.

"Good idea." Crispy nods.

"When was the last time anyone saw Apollo?" I ask.

"I checked on the animals at lunchtime right after I got out of surgery," Mom says. "That was around noon."

"We got home from school at about three thirty." I check my spy watch. "We noticed him missing about an hour later. The door to Apollo's pen was closed. So, he didn't just wander out." I get up to inspect the empty enclosure. "Someone let him out and then shut the door again."

"Or someone stole him," Crispy says.

"Stole Apollo!" Mom's eyes get wide. "Why would someone steal a cougar kitten?"

I bend down and examine the sawdust around the entrance to Apollo's pen. A bit of metal winks up at me. I stir the dust with the toe of my boot and then squat to get a closer look. "Hey, I found something." I pick up a barrette—using a tissue from the pocket of my spy vest—and hold it out in the palm of my hand.

"Evidence!" Crispy jumps up to take a look. "Whose is it?"

It's not Mom's. She has one of those short haircuts that makes her look like a really cute boy, especially when she wears her overalls, which is most of the time (except when she's wearing her blue scrubs at the vet clinic).

"Not mine." I hold the barrette up by its clasp and take a closer look. It's about two inches long and has a strong fastener. "I'd never wear such silly pink flowers." A strand of black hair is stuck in the latch. "Aha! Now we're getting somewhere." I turn to Crispy and say, "Turn on the overhead lights."

"What is it?" Crispy asks. He lifts Freddie out of his jacket and lets the ferret climb onto his shoulder. Then my brother sprints across the barn to the light switch before dashing back to check out my evidence.

Freddie sniffs at the barrette and reaches a paw toward the clip. When I pull it away from him, he toots in protest. He's always stealing stuff and ferreting it away in some secret hiding place.

"Don't move," I say. "There may be more evidence at the scene of the crime."

"Crime?" Mom asks. "*Someone* let Apollo out of his pen and forgot to close the gate to the petting zoo, and Apollo wandered out." She looks from me to Crispy. "He'd better turn up soon, or *someone* will be in a lot of trouble."

"*Someone* isn't me," I say, glaring at Crispy.

"If we don't find him in the next hour, I'm calling Animal Control," Mom says.

"No! You can't!" I stop my search and give Mom a pleading look. "Please don't."

"I have to," Mom says. "A cougar—even a kitten—on the loose in the suburbs is serious business."

"But they'll shut us down!"

"That's why we have to notify them. So they *won't* shut us down." The color drains from Mom's face. I hope she's not getting sick again. "We have one hour to find him, then I'm calling."

"Don't worry, Mom." I walk over and put my hand on her shoulder. "I'll find him."

I redouble my resolve to find Apollo before that glorified dogcatcher Pinkerton Killjoy captures him and closes us down. I go back to the evidence and hold up the barrette.

"That hair clip probably fell off some girl's ponytail last weekend." Mom reaches for the clip. "We had a pretty full house."

Rather than lecture her on getting fingerprints on the barrette, I hand it over in a tissue . . . *after* I remove the strand and seal the hair inside a plastic baggie. She's my mom after all.

Using a rake to sift through the sawdust, I continue searching for evidence. *Aha!* "I found something else!"

Crispy runs over to investigate. "What is it?"

I hold up a square mechanical pencil.

"What's that doing here?" Mom asks. She grabs it out of my hand and examines it. "Your dad's pencil."

Dad's a lawyer, and he has a whole stash of mechanical pencils and fancy pens. Mom pockets the pencil. She just doesn't get it. Anything can be a clue.

I shrug and go back to my search. It's crucial to sweep the crime scene as soon as possible so clues don't go stale.

Mom is wringing her hands, pacing the full length of the barn. I'm worried about her. After Dad left, she lost so much weight she almost disappeared. I can't let that happen again. I won't let her lose everything again. If I don't find Apollo, we'll lose the cub and the whole petting zoo. That would kill Mom and Crispy. They both love animals more than anything in the world. That familiar itchy prickling starts scratching at my eyes again.

I've just got to solve the mystery of our missing cub before Agent Killjoy gets his grubby hands on him. There are only thirty-seven more minutes before Mom has to call Animal Control. My stomach sours at the thought of our poor little cub in the back of Agent Killjoy's Animal Control van. My heart is pounding like a bass drum.

Calm down, Kassy. Concentrate. Use your brain, you must. I imagine Jedi Master Yoda's voice in my head. *A detective, you are. Follow clues, you must.*

Something else flashes from the sawdust. I pick it up. "Hey, Crispy, here's your missing button." I hand the metal button to my brother.

He fingers the spot on his wool coat where the button should be. "Thanks."

I kick the sawdust. I need real evidence, not Crispy's missing buttons. I need clues to help us find Apollo before the evil dogcatcher captures him and takes him away from us for good, then shuts down the petting zoo.

4
TOO MANY CLUES

AFTER SCOURING THE ENTIRE PETTING ZOO inside and out, here's a list of the evidence I found at the crime scene (not including Crispy's missing button and a half-eaten stick of black licorice, no doubt also my brother's): one barrette (with strand of black hair), one mechanical pencil (probably Dad's, confiscated by Mom but later cleverly taken from her pocket by me), one gold lapel pin, a pair of eyeglasses, one leather driving glove, a page torn from a coloring book, one filthy white sock, one doggy tug toy, and an unidentified neon green plastic thing.

I carefully arrange the evidence on the breakfast table. There's so much that the stuff barely fits. I take out my notebook and pen to describe every item in detail. Crispy and Flatulent

Freddie are sitting next to me, watching. Freddie jumps on the table, sniffs the tug toy, then grabs the pencil and runs off. I narrow my eyes at Crispy, who catches the ferret and retrieves the evidence.

I catalog and analyze the clues. First, we have the barrette with possibly the most important clue of all: the strand of black hair. It must belong to someone with hair long enough to be tied into a ponytail or a man bun. And this person has black hair. I hold the baggie containing the strand up to the light. The hair is thick with a slight curl. "We're looking for someone with long, black, curly hair," I say, jotting it down in my notebook. I open the baggie and sniff. *Whew, smells like lavender perfume.*

"Agent Killjoy has black hair," Crispy says.

"Agent Pinky Killjoy's hair is brown, and it's too short to be tied in a ponytail." What kind of name is *Pinky*? I call him

Stinkerton, or *Stinky* for short. He may be stinky, but he doesn't smell like lavender.

I hold the mechanical pencil between my thumb and forefinger, then set it on a paper towel. I take out my fingerprint powder. I put down paper towels first because Mom doesn't like it when I make a mess. Of course, she makes them all the time with her experiments on the kitchen counters. Half the time, our kitchen looks like a science lab. "Do as I say and not as I do," she says whenever I point this out to her.

When I swirl the brush in the powder and then lightly brush the pencil, some partial prints appear. They're definitely adult-sized fingers.

"Are those Dad's fingerprints?" Crispy asks, his elbows on the table, chin leaning on his hands. Freddie is lying across his head like a fur cap.

I ignore them and put the pencil back in its place.

The gold lapel pin is an interesting clue. It's shaped like a curly letter *M*. "Our perpetrator's name might begin with *M*," I say as I pick the pin up and turn it over. I take the magnifying

glass from my spy vest and examine the back of the pin. There's a piece of beige fuzz on the clasp. I pick it off and drop it into another baggie. "And they may wear a beige wool jacket."

"Morpheus!" Crispy sits up, and Freddie scrambles to hold on to his hair.

"*Malarkey, mugwump, mudpack, muktuk, mollusk, muddlehead,*" I say, listing all the *M* words that come to mind (even though I haven't gotten that far in the dictionary).

"Morpheus wears beige wool."

"Morpheus is a pony and *wears* nothing, unless you've been putting clothes on him again."

Crispy just shrugs.

"Nice try, though." I force a smile. "A pony kidnapping a cougar cub." I shake my head. Sometimes I think my brother is mental, another *M* word. "These glasses look familiar." I hold up the purple specs.

"Really?" Crispy reaches for them.

I jerk them away. "There's a black strap attached to their arms." I examine the safety strap.

As if in warning, Freddie swivels toward the door and toots.

Mom bursts into the kitchen waving the telephone book. "I can't find him anywhere." She points the book at my brother. "Perseus Charon O'Roarke, what have you done with Apollo?" Why do parents always use your whole name when they're upset? No wonder everyone hates their middle name.

"Nothing." Crispy buries his face in Freddie's fur.

"Kassandra Urania O'Roarke."

I cringe.

"Did you leave the door to his enclosure open when you fed him this morning?"

"No!" *How could she even think I'd be so careless?*

"You're always half asleep, wandering around in a dream. Are you sure?"

"Yes, I'm sure." I grit my teeth.

Mom grabs the phone. "The hour is up."

"Don't call Animal Control!" I'm fighting tears again. "Please, Mom. If Agent Killjoy finds Apollo, he'll take him away from us and close down the petting zoo." I hold my breath until the tears stop. I don't know why I'm crying so much these days. Ever since Dad left, everything makes me want to cry. Another reason to train my brain to think like a detective. So I won't cry. Instead, I'll figure stuff out, solve crimes, and become a doer. Then maybe Dad will come home.

"Kassy'll find Apollo," Crispy says. "She's gonna crack the case and write the best story for the school paper." He grins at me. "She's gonna win a prize."

I'm embarrassed by his confidence in me. Sometimes my baby brother is okay. I sniffle.

"I'm going to give it my best shot." I pick up the tug toy.

After making the dreaded call, Mom drops the phone, marches over, and snatches the toy out of my hand. "That's filthy. Where'd you get it?"

"It's a clue." I tighten my lips.

Mom rolls her eyes. "It's Zeus's old chew rope." Zeus is our golden retriever. He lives at Dad's house in Nashville. Yeah, Dad got custody of the dog, and Mom got us. At least Zeus is house-broken. I don't know if I can say the same for Crispy. Just joking.

Mom dangles the toy over the trash can.

"No." I dash over and grab it just in time.

"What do you want with that old thing?"

"It's evidence." I place the tug toy back on the table.

"Watch your brother. I'm going back to the woods to search for Apollo again." Mom gathers up her wool coat and a flashlight. "Don't leave the house. If you get hungry, there are some kale chips in the cupboard."

My brother and I glance at each other. Even Crispy draws the line at kale.

"Can I come with you?" Crispy asks.

"No. Stay here," Mom says as she slams the door and disappears. Maybe she's not as unflappable as I thought.

Once Mom is gone, I take up my pen and notebook again. "Where were we?" I have to focus on the evidence to figure out what happened to Apollo. That's the only way I can save him and our petting zoo. No use doing something until you know what it is you're doing.

Crispy points to the sock.

"Right. One white sock." I take the tweezers from my spy vest and pinch them around the top of the sock . . . not because I'm worried about fingerprints but who wants to touch someone else's stinky sock? I sit down and hold the sock up to my shoe. "Whoever this belongs to is smaller than I am. Hold up your foot." I size up the sock against Crispy's foot. "Somewhere in between your foot and mine. That means it probably belongs to someone around nine or ten years old." I place the sock back on the table. "How could someone lose their sock and not notice?"

"I do it all the time," Crispy says. "So does Freddie."

"Freddie's socks are permanent."

"Not when I use your dolls' socks."

"What?"

"His feet get cold."

Whatever! I don't want to argue with Crispy about messing with my dolls, so instead I write in my notebook: *One sock belonging to a ten-year-old. Very dirty. (The sock is dirty—not the ten-year-old.)*

"What about these eyeglasses?" When I pick them up and look through them, I feel like I'm on a boat on the ocean during a storm. Everything sways, and I get seasick. "Our culprit's blind as a bat." I still think I've seen these glasses someplace before . . . but where? "These glasses are way stronger than mine." I put my own glasses back on and my stomach settles down.

"Bats aren't blind. Just because they use their ears to find their way in the dark doesn't mean they can't see."

"I know. Okay, I doubt our suspect's a bat."

"Too bad. Bat poop is very useful."

"What do you know about bat guano?"

"We learned about bats in school," Crispy says. "Bats are cool."

I hate bats, but I humor him. "Yes, very cool." Growing up on a ranch, I'm not supposed to be afraid of bats, but I have to admit they creep me out big-time. I'm glad our suspect is not a bat, even if their poop is the main ingredient in Doritos.

My stomach growls. I fetch the kale chips from the cupboard and tear open the bag. The wrinkly green "chips" look like skink skin. Skinks are little lizards native to Tennessee. We catch them at our pond . . . our ex-pond.

When I hold the chip bag out to Crispy, Freddie dives in, and kale chips go flying across the kitchen.

Biscuits and gravy! Mom picks this moment to walk into the kitchen. *Crunch, crunch, crunch.* She steps on kale chips and scowls.

"Kassandra Urania O'Roarke, what's going on in here?"

"Freddie jumped—" I start to say, but Mom interrupts.

"Don't blame Freddie. He's merely a *Mustela putorius furo*, with a brain the size of a walnut." That's Mom's way of saying *ferret*.

"But the little weasel tried—"

"Don't call Freddie a *weasel*," Crispy chimes in.

I give up. I go down on my hands and knees to scoop up the kale chips. I'm almost hungry enough to eat them off the floor. "Did you find Apollo?" I ask, glancing up at Mom.

"No. Now take that dirty garbage off the table so we can have dinner." Mom takes a bunch of containers out of the refrigerator and snaps their lids off.

I wonder what leftovers we get tonight—vegan mac and cheese or gluten-free spinach enchiladas.

"This *garbage* is evidence." I make air quotes with my fingers. Mom puts her hands on her hips and glares at me. As a peace offering, I hold up the bag of kale chips I picked up off the floor. Mom grabs it and pitches it into the trash.

When she turns her back, I rescue the evidence and sprint up to my room before Mom makes me throw it all away.

5

THE MEANING OF LIFE

THE NEXT DAY IN STUDY HALL, I review my notes from last night. Since I've already finished my math homework, I hide my green flip notebook inside my math textbook and study the clues I've gathered so far.

Looks like our suspect is a ten-year-old with black hair . . . or else our golden retriever, Zeus, or Dad. Zeus can open the gate with his snout, but why would he kidnap Apollo? He likes cats, but not that much. Anyway, how would he get all the way out to Lemontree Heights from downtown Nashville? It's a ten-minute drive. Plus, he doesn't drive and wouldn't have bus fare because he's a dog. *Holy harebrained!* I'm starting to think like Crispy. I shake the cobwebs out of my head.

Why would Dad kidnap Apollo? If he misses him, he could just come visit. I can't see Dad doing a thing like that. He has the means—a car and bus fare—but he doesn't have a motive. Does he?

So that leaves the ten-year-old with black hair. Do I know any ten-year-olds who have a thing for cougar cubs? I accidently chew on my pencil. A bad habit, I know, but it feels so nice when the wood surrenders to my teeth.

"Hey, Carrot Top, whatcha doing?"

Oh no. Butler Patel.

I hate it when people call me *Carrot Top*. I don't like *Ginger* much either. My hair is auburn, not orange or yellow! At least he doesn't call me *Four-Eyes* or *Squirrel-Face* like some of the eighth-grade creeps do.

Butler sits behind me in honors math class and pulls on my ponytail. He has shaggy black hair, brown eyes, and bushy black eyebrows. His feet look like a clown's. Mom says he'll grow into them. Yeah, if he becomes a giant.

"Hey, Butt-ler." I fake smile.

"What's that?" Butler points to my notebook.

"I'm working on a case."

The bell rings. It's time for English class. I stuff my textbook and notebook into my backpack and scoot out of my desk. I'm walking fast to try to get away from Butler. It's no use. His legs are longer than mine. He's stuck to my side like a tick on a bunny's ear.

"What case?" he asks, keeping up with me step for step.

"None of your wax."

"Maybe I can help."

"You can help by leaving me alone." I glance over and fake smile again. Butler gives me a hangdog look and heads into our honors English classroom. He slumps into his desk. I hurry across the room to mine, scoot into my chair, and unpack my stuff.

Apart from the weird boys, middle school has some advantages over grade school. For one, I don't have to sit for hours at the same desk in the same classroom staring out the same window at the same hackberry tree. And I get to learn about cool subjects. Every Friday at lunch, a teacher gives an extra class on weird topics, and anyone who's interested can go. Last week, we learned about philosophy, which is about the meaning of life. If I don't become a detective or a spy, maybe I'll become a philosopher. That way I can discover why I was born. There must be a reason. I can't just be a random event, like the fire burning down the barn or Smelly Kelly catching the vandal. Can I?

Since Dad left, sometimes I wish I hadn't been born. When he lectures me with disappointment in his eyes, I want to apologize for being born. But the words won't come out. What if it's my fault Dad left? What if it's my fault Mom had the nervous breakdown? What if it's my fault Crispy burned down the barn and now Apollo is lost?

I quietly slip my emergency granola bar from my spy vest and try to push those thoughts out of my head. I glance up to see if Mrs. Cheever is watching me. When she turns to write *Harper Lee, To Kill a Mockingbird* on the blackboard, I rip the wrapper open with my teeth, then hide the bar in my lap until the wrapper's crinkling blends into all the other noises from the classroom. Whenever Mrs. Cheever's back is turned, I take another bite of my granola bar.

After the lunch bell rings, I head for the biology lab to use the microscope. I want to examine the hair I found at the crime scene. My biology teacher, Mr. Potter, is sitting in the front of the room at his desk, munching on a sandwich. He looks like a chubby chipmunk wearing wire-rim glasses. When I enter the room, he looks up from his lunch with a question mark on his face. I smile—for real this time—and pick up my pace.

I love the biology lab, with its long metal tables, little sinks, microscopes, and glass slides. The lab has a sharp, pungent smell like Alka-Seltzer. Some days, though, it smells like rotten eggs. Those are good days to avoid the lab.

Another reason I like to come to the lab is to talk to Mr. Potter. He takes philosophy courses in night school. That's how I heard about philosophy. He's the one who talked about it last week at the lunchtime lecture. He says philosophers ask questions like "How do we know this chair is real?" and "How do we know other people really exist and aren't just dreams or figments of our own imagination?"

I'm about to ask Mr. Potter if I can use one of the microscopes when the door creaks open and I turn around. *Holy headache!* It's Butler. I wish *he* were just a figment of my imagination.

"Ms. O'Roarke, Mr. Patel. Are you here for the extra-credit project?" Mr. Potter's bushy sideburns jiggle when he talks. He looks like he has Brillo Pads stuck to the sides of his face.

"Yes," Butler says. "Kassy and I are working together."

Catfish and gravy! I wish Butler would leave me alone. Now I'm stuck with him. "Is it okay if we use one of the microscopes?"

I ask. "I'm . . . We're working on a special project." It's almost the truth. I am working on a special project—namely, finding our missing cougar cub before the evil Animal Control agent Stinky Killjoy catches him.

"That's right." Butler's brown cheeks turn pink. "A very special project."

I try not to glare at him.

"Sure. I'm glad you kids are interested in science." Mr. Potter points to a lab station. "You can work at table three. Collaboration is important in science. It's great you kids are working together."

Bang! An explosion stops me in my tracks. Kelly Finkelman is giggling behind her hand. Her lab partner, Jessica Dobey, blinks like a deer in the headlights, her eyebrows singed. They're both cheerleaders and too cool for school.

"Curses!" Mr. Potter storms over to their table. "What happened?"

Stifling her giggles, Smelly Kelly says, "It was an accident."

Tears are welling in Jessica's eyes.

"Are you okay?" Mr. Potter asks. "Curses! Your eyebrows."

"Come on," I say to Butler and head toward table three. The acrid smell of burning hair overpowers the Alka-Seltzer and takes over the lab.

At table three, I slip the baggie from the pocket of my spy vest.

"What's that?" Butler asks.

"A hair."

"Whose hair?"

"That's what we're about to find out."

"Wow. Cool." He puts his hands on the table and leans down for a closer look at the baggie.

"I found it at the crime scene," I say, picking up the baggie and carefully removing the hair.

"Whoa. What crime?" he asks.

Let's see . . . theft, kidnapping, possibly costing us the petting zoo. Without a word, I place the hair between two slides and set it under the lens of the microscope. The hair reveals some interesting information. "*Whoa* is right." My pulse is racing.

"Can I look?" Butler asks.

"Okay. But don't disturb the evidence." I step aside so he can take a peek.

"So, whose is it?" he asks.

"Not *who*, but *what*," I say. "See how the medulla is thick and the cuticle is made up of ovoid scales?"

"*Medulla? Ovoid?*" he asks.

"*Medulla* means *middle.* And the cuticle is the outer layer. This hair's cuticle has scales like fish scales, only they're oval." I yank out one of Butler's hairs and slide it under the microscope.

"Ouch!" He puts his hand to his head.

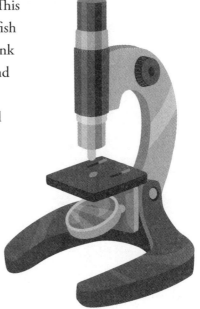

"A human hair has smaller, less distinct scales, more like waves or flakes. See the different colors in the first hair? Now look at your hair."

"Wow. How can one black hair have so many

colors and such an amazing pattern of scales?" When he smiles at me, dimples sprout on his cheeks. "My hair looks like snakeskin."

"Human hair is more constant in color and less constant in the shape of the scales." I slide the hair out from under the microscope and drop it back into the baggie. Good thing Mom taught me everything I know about animal hair, animal tracks, and animal poop. Like Mom, I know my animals.

I look up at Butler. "This, my friend, is not human hair."

When I call him *my friend,* Butler straightens to his full gangly height and beams down at me.

"It was a figure of speech," I say, my face hot.

"So, it's animal hair?"

"Dog hair, to be precise."

6

FREDDIE'S ALMOST FLATTENED

WHEN THE LAST BELL RINGS, I jump up from my desk. I'm in a hurry to get back home to the evidence. Now I know the hair is dog hair and not human hair, and that's a good lead. I need to reexamine the clues and figure out who kidnapped Apollo. I'm sure he didn't just wander off. Someone took him. And I'm going to find out who. Whoever took him, I hope they know how to take care of a cougar kitten. Poor little guy.

I skirt the lockers, trying not to make eye contact with the cheerleaders and football jocks hanging around the hallway after school. Not that they would ever stoop to acknowledge my existence, except maybe to pick me up and throw me against the lockers. A couple of the football dudes think tossing me around is fun, but it makes me want to throw up. It's terrifying. That's why I go out of my way to stay away from them. It's the only way to survive middle school. I stick to myself and my books. I guess you could say Nancy Drew and Harry Potter are my best friends. Crispy's got his furry friends, and I've got my fictional friends. Sad but true.

In my rush this morning, I forgot my hat and scarf. The wind stings my ears, and my fingers are stiff. I'm not used to cold temperatures in Tennessee, especially not in May. *Poor Apollo. What if he did just wander off and he's lost?* I hope he's warm wherever he is . . . and I hope he has food. He's used to people feeding him. How can he survive on his own? My stomach flips just thinking about the little guy out in the woods by himself.

Let's see . . . it's been about twenty-four hours since he went missing. I wonder how long cougar cubs can survive without food. He should be able to get water from puddles. But what will he eat? I hope he knows how to hunt. All he's had to do for the past two months is amble over to his food bowl.

I'm speed walking toward Crispy's elementary school. I've got to round him up, get home, and retrace every inch of the property—even if we have to trespass on Mr. and Mrs. Busybody's land (which rightfully belongs to us anyway).

Speak of the deviled egg, here comes Crispy strolling up the sidewalk with Freddie peeking out from the neck of his sweater.

"You're supposed to wait for me. You're going to get us both in trouble."

"I had a brainstorm."

"Brain fog, more like," I say under my breath.

"I recognize the barrette," he says.

"Really?" If anyone knows a dog who wears a barrette, it's Crispy.

"It's Ronny's."

"Ronny?" I ask.

"Our sister," he answers.

"Veronica is not our sister." I exhale out loud.

"Dad says she is."

"Dad and Mari aren't married, so she's not even our *step*sister . . . yet." I cringe thinking about calling Rotten Ronny *sister*.

Thanks to Crispy's arson, now we only see Dad on the weekends. His skinny girlfriend tries to butter us up with homemade cookies and coconut flan. Crispy doesn't have the strength to resist. But I do. Crispy, the little traitor, loves swiveling on Dad's barstools and stuffing his mouth with cookies like everything is fine.

Believe me, things are far from fine. I don't even know if Dad likes us anymore. I used to just assume he did. He had to. He was our dad. Now, he lives with another family, and we're just visitors.

"Why is it called *step*sister?" Crispy asks.

"'Cause we ought to step on her face?"

"No, really."

"In Old English, *steop* meant *orphan*. Widows remarried and their kids were called *stepkids*." Okay, along with the dictionary, sometimes I read the encyclopedia too. I like to learn stuff. Whatever else gets taken away from me—our pond, the ranch, my dad—no one can take away the stuff in my head. My brain is my secret weapon.

I pull the baggie from my pocket and hold it up. "The hair on this barrette isn't human. While Ronny's probably an alien, I doubt she's a dog."

"A dog?"

"Yeah, the hair on the barrette is dog hair. Come on." I grab Crispy's hand and yank it. "We've got to find Apollo before something bad happens to him."

"You think something bad's gonna to happen to Apollo?" Crispy's voice breaks.

"No, Potato Chip. We're going to find him *before* then." I head for the crosswalk.

Holy hound catcher! Who do I see across the street? Agent Stinkerton Killjoy in his yellow Animal Control van. He's stopped at the intersection in front of our school, waiting for the stoplight to change. I pull on Crispy's arm and then break into a run.

"Where are we going?" he yells, trying to keep up.

"Look." I point at Killjoy's van. "We've got to make sure Apollo's not in the back of that van."

"Apollo," Crispy squeaks as I dig my fingernails into his hand. Freddie squeaks too —and not just from his weasel snout, if you know what I mean. Amazing he never does that at school. I can't believe Crispy hasn't gotten busted for bringing a ferret to class.

By the time we look both ways and cross the street, the traffic light has changed to green, and Agent Killjoy is on the move. We've got to catch up to that van and find out if Apollo's inside. I drop Crispy's hand and take off running as fast as I can. I glance over my shoulder. Crispy is falling behind. I consider waiting, but the evil Killjoy is getting away.

As I cross the street, I glance back again. *Oh no!* It's Freddie. He's gaining on me. He must have jumped out of Crispy's sweater. Freddie doesn't know to look both ways before crossing the road.

My heart leaps into my throat. A car is coming straight for Freddie. The ferret stops in the middle of the street, looking confused. Crispy is running after Freddie instead of looking out for cars. *Please don't let him run out into the street.* "Percy!" I yell. "Watch for cars!"

"Freddie!" I shout. "Please, Freddie . . . please, please, please!" I scream as I sprint to save him.

I'm hyperventilating, and I'm going to barf. Crispy is still running. Freddie is still frozen. The car is just a couple of feet from Freddie. "*Stop!*" I bellow.

Like magic, the car stops. *Brussels sprouts!* I almost peed my pants. Crispy and I descend on Freddie, who's still standing in the middle of the road. My little brother snatches him up, kisses his head, and tucks the ferret back into his sweater.

I'm totally freaking out, and Crispy's cool as a cucumber. I hope Mom doesn't find out. She'll have puppies if she finds out I left Crispy alone on a busy street.

My brother waves at the driver of the SUV.

"Hey, Kassy," a familiar voice says from the back window. It's Butler Patel.

Holy hot rod! Butler's older brother is driving. *What's he doing behind the wheel?*

"I didn't know you could drive." *What a stupid thing to say.*

"I'm seventeen," Butler's brother says with a smirk. "I'm a pro." With his wavy black hair, dark eyes, and pearly white teeth, he looks like an older version of Butler, except instead of wearing nice slacks and a polo shirt, he's wearing holey jeans and a frayed flannel shirt. *Holy highlight!* Is that a tattoo on his wrist? I stare at the red-and-black snake inked on his arm.

Butler smiles at me and asks, "You guys need a ride?"

I'm about to say *nah* when I realize Butler and his scary older brother might be our only hope of catching up to the Animal Control van and finding Apollo.

"Come on, Crispy." I open the back door of the SUV, shove my little brother and Freddie inside, and dive in after them. "Follow that van!"

7

AGENT STINKERTON KILLJOY

"*FOLLOW THAT VAN!*" I shout again.

"What's going on?" asks Butler's tattooed brother, Oliver.

"Animal Control picked up our cat by mistake." I don't mention that the cat is a cougar cub. "We want to catch that van and get him back."

Oliver cranks his head around and slowly accelerates. At this rate, we're never going to catch up to the evil Killjoy and his Animal Control van.

"Can you go faster?" I ask. "We've got to catch that van."

Oliver glances at me in the rearview mirror. "Is this the girl you've been telling me about?" he asks Butler. "You're right about her hair. Wow. So red." He turns around and smiles at me. "She's a cutie."

Butler's face turns pink, and he glares over at his brother.

Shrimp and grits! Has Butler been talking to his brother about me? My face gets hot, and my chest feels weird, like it's full of ants or something. No time to think about that now. We've got to catch Killjoy. "Hurry! We've got to save our cat."

"Kassy is writing a story about our cougar cub for the school newspaper," Crispy chimes in.

"A mountain lion?" Butler asks.

"A mountain lion is a cat," I say and then bare my teeth at Crispy. He must think I'm about to bite. He puts his head inside his sweater and whispers something to Freddie.

"What's that musky smell?" Oliver asks. "Reminds me of a girl I knew back home."

I stifle a laugh. What kind of girls did Butler's brother hang out with that smelled like farting ferrets?

"Our lion might be in trouble," I say. "Can you step on it?"

Oliver glances back at me in the rearview mirror. "Don't worry. I'll catch him." When he stomps on the gas, the car

jolts into high gear. I lurch forward, catching myself against the back of the front seat.

"The van's stopped at the light," Crispy says. "We can catch up if we hurry."

"Righto." Oliver steps on it again. The SUV hiccups and then zooms down the street.

Kelly Finkelman and Jessica Dobey are at the corner up ahead. As we whiz past, they stand there in their matching miniskirts, staring with their mouths open like beached hogfish. I smile and wave.

"He's pulling into the Pool and Splash." I point toward our favorite summer hangout. When it's scorching hot in August, there's nothing like the giant water slide to cool off. Next to the Pool and Splash is a public park with picnic tables and a playground.

"Now what?" Butler asks.

"We check out the back of that van."

Oliver signals and then pulls into the parking lot. We watch while Agent Killjoy tiptoes toward the water slide, carrying a giant pole with a loop at the end. With his beaky nose and long beige coattails flapping in the wind, he looks like a potbellied stork tramping across the grass.

"That poor little puppy," Crispy says. "We've got to save him." He points toward the park, where a little fur ball is scampering across the playground. Agent Killjoy is trying to catch the puppy with the loop on the end of the long pole.

"Just concentrate on saving Apollo," I say as I open the car door. "Come on."

"Thanks for the ride," Crispy says as he steps out of the car.

"Yeah, thanks," I say. Then I take off running toward the van.

Crispy and Freddie are right behind me. I glance around to make sure Killjoy is out of sight and then push the back-door handle of the van. It's locked. "Try the driver's door," I tell Crispy.

He runs around to the front of the van. I peek around to see him jiggle the door handle. "Locked." He shrugs.

I wish I'd brought my slim jim. No, not a pepperoni. It's a long metal tool for getting into locked cars. Mom is forgetful and locks herself out of her Jeep a lot. But the slim jim is too long to fit in my spy vest, so Crispy and I use it as a slingshot to propel his *Star Wars* LEGOs into orbit.

I join Crispy at the driver's-side door. Shielding my eyes with one hand, I peer into the window of the van. *Now what?*

Crispy runs around to the passenger side of the van. "It's unlocked!" he hollers as he opens the door.

"Unlock the back door!" I yell.

"Watch out!" Butler shouts.

What's he still doing here? The ants in my chest start doing some kind of war dance behind my rib cage.

"The dogcatcher—he's coming!" Butler points toward the park.

My mind is racing, but my feet are frozen as I watch Crispy dash to the back of the van.

"Hey, what are you doing?" A gruff voice startles me. "Get away from my van." Agent Pinkerton Killjoy is barreling toward us from the other end of the parking lot.

Crispy opens the back door and disappears. I crank my head around the van, but I can't see him. He must have climbed inside the back of the van.

"Crispy, get out of there!" I yell. "Killjoy will be here any second." As I round the front of the van, a rough hand grabs my wrist. My heart is beating like a bass drum. I can almost hear it thudding in my chest.

"What do you think you're doing?" *Holy halitosis!* Agent Killjoy's breath could knock over a horse. "You're that O'Roarke girl."

"And you're Animal Control agent Killjoy." I stiffen under his grip.

Killjoy looks confused, like he doesn't understand English. He opens his mouth and then closes it again.

I scrunch up my nose in disgust. *That* he understands.

He tightens his grip on my arm and drags me around to the passenger side of the van. "Like I told your mother, one of these days, I'm going to close down Lemontree Petting Zoo. Petting zoos are for domestic animals, not wild ones."

"Unhand me, you brute!" I shout. (I heard that on TV). "I have rights, and you're an animal cop, not a person police."

He looks at me like I'm speaking Klingon.

"Need some help?" Butler appears out of nowhere.

"I can take care of myself." I wrench my arm away from Killjoy. *But what about Crispy? Can I take care of him too?* "Crispy!" I shout.

"I'm warning you, stay away from my van." Killjoy waves his nasty dog-catching pole at us. "If I get one more complaint about an escaped animal, or if one of those wild animals harms someone, I'll put Lemontree Petting Zoo out of business for good."

I feel like socking him in the mouth. "Not if I can help it." I spit out the words.

"Why are you looking in my van? Did you lose one of your animals again?"

Aha! So he hasn't found Apollo.

"Come on, Kassy," Butler puts his hand on my shoulder. "Let's go."

"If you lost one of those wild animals again, I'm going to find it. And when I do . . ."

I think the ants have moved up to my brain and switched into full attack mode. My mind is racing all over the place as I follow Butler back to the SUV. His brother is in the driver's seat, listening to hip-hop music and nodding to the beat.

"Oh no!" I watch in horror as Agent Killjoy speeds away. "Crispy." My voice cracks. "My brother's still in the back of the van."

8
DOG BISCUITS

I HAVE NO CHOICE BUT TO GO HOME without Crispy. How am I going to tell Mom I lost my little brother? I wince when I think of what Stinkerton Killjoy will do when he finds Crispy in the back of his van. A shiver runs up my spine, and my whole body goes cold. Everything is crashing down on me. The fire, Dad leaving, Apollo missing, Crispy trapped in that van. For the first time in my life, I'm scared, really scared. Not for myself but for Crispy. He may be a pest sometimes, but he's got a big heart—too big for his own good. I shouldn't have told him to check the back of the van. It's my fault he's Killjoy's prisoner. I've got to rescue him. But how?

"I guess you'd better take me home," I say.

"Want to call your mom?" Butler offers me his cell phone. If Butler Patel has a phone, why can't I? Everyone at school—except me—has a phone. Mom says I'm too young, but come on, I'm almost a teenager.

"Nah. I'd better tell her in person," I say. If I call her, I'll have to explain why I'm not home yet and why Crispy's not with me. In my twelve years on the planet, I've learned that it's best to rehearse my story before I present it to Mom. Dad says, "Reason persuades; it doesn't scream and wail." I think that's just his way of telling me to shut up.

"Are you okay?" Butler holds out a silver container filled with bright orange candies. They look like shiny worms and chalky rectangular tiles. "Here. Some sweets are just what you need."

I doubt Mom would agree, but I take a tile. I could use a boost before I face the kale chips at home. "What is it?"

"*Badam barfi*. My mom made it." When Butler smiles, his face lights up. "She's opening a bakery."

"Did you say *barfy*?" I'm about to take my first bite when a rap on the window gives me a start. I drop the treat on the floor. When I look up, I see Crispy outside the car holding a fur ball covered in mud.

"Crispy!" I've never been so happy to see my little brother in my life.

My brother smiles and holds up the muddy puppy like a trophy. "I saved him."

I open the door, and Crispy climbs into the back seat and cradles the puppy. "Poor thing's hurt," he says. "Maybe he stepped on a sharp rock or something." Crispy holds up the pooch's bleeding paw.

"How'd you escape?" I ask. I examine the wound. It doesn't look too bad.

"Escape?"

"How'd you get out of Killjoy's van?"

"I never got in." Crispy shrugs. "I saw Apollo wasn't there, so I went to rescue this little guy." He snuggles the wriggling puppy.

"Here, wrap this around his foot." Oliver unties a blue bandanna from around his head and hands it back over the seat. "I don't want blood all over the car."

"Let's get him home. Mom will fix him up," I say.

"Where do you live?" Oliver asks.

"I know where Kassy lives," Butler says. "Lemontree Animal Hospital and Petting Zoo."

Wait. What? Butler knows where I live? Is he a stalker or something?

Crispy starts squirming and looking wildly around the inside of the SUV, panic on his face.

"What's wrong?" I ask.

"Where's Freddie?"

"Don't you have him?" I look around, but I already know Freddie isn't in the car. If he were, I'd smell him. "When was the last time you saw him?"

"He was in my sweater when I checked the back of the van. Then I saw the puppy under a picnic table and I ran to save the little guy. Maybe Freddie fell out when I ran?"

"Does he come when you call him?" Butler asks.

"Will you please hold the puppy while we look for Freddie?" Crispy passes the puppy into the front seat. Butler takes it in both hands and hugs the wriggling fur ball to his chest.

"Let's spread out and search the park," I say.

Butler hands the puppy to his brother. "I'll help search."

Oliver starts singing a lullaby to the puppy, but I can't understand the words. Maybe he's not so scary after all.

Butler, Crispy, and I search every inch of the public park but see no sign of Freddie. I crawl on my knees, sniffing like an animal to see if I can smell him. But all I smell is the scent of green grass, spicy pine needles, and earthy dried dog poo. Even with my super-duper sense of smell, I don't detect Freddie's distinctive musk. *Nope.* Freddie is nowhere to be found. I stand up and brush at the grass stains on the knees of my jeans. Mom's going to love those. *Not.*

"Poor Freddie." Crispy has tears in his eyes. "He's my best friend."

"Don't worry. We'll find him," I say, trying to be brave for Crispy's sake.

Holy horror-struck! I have an idea, a sick and scary idea. "Was there any food in the back of the Animal Control van?"

"There was a pile of dog biscuits," Crispy answers. We look at each other in horror. "Oh no!" we say in unison. Freddie loves dog biscuits.

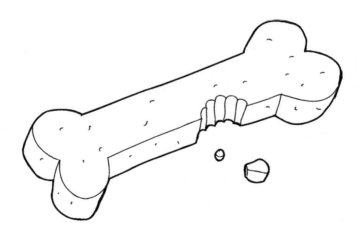

9

REVIEWING THE CLUES

AS SOON AS THE PATEL BROTHERS DROP US OFF, Crispy and I
rush into the clinic with the injured puppy. The clinic kind
of freaks me out with its polished metal surfaces. The smell
of bleach covers up other more organic smells coming from
the dog cages. And it's always really cold in here. Even in win-
ter, the air conditioning is blasting. I hardly ever come in here
unless I have to. Anyway, technically, we're not allowed in the
clinic except in the case of an emergency. A bleeding puppy—
and a captured ferret—count as emergencies.

A vet tech in blue scrubs tells us Mom's in surgery and
can't be disturbed. Crispy hands the injured puppy to the tech.
We follow her into an exam room, where she disinfects and

bandages the hurt paw. The tech scans the pup for a microchip. *Whew.* He has a chip. The tech uses a computer to locate his owner's phone number and places the call. Turns out, the puppy's people live across from the park, and they've been looking all over for their fur baby. We leave the puppy with the tech and head into our house. Our small brick house is attached to the vet clinic, and the side door to the clinic leads right into our kitchen.

I sit down at the kitchen table to wait for Mom. Crispy does the same. "What about Freddie?" he whines.

"Don't worry. Mom can get him back." At least I hope so. "She'll be out of surgery soon, and then we can fetch Freddie."

In the meantime, I need to get back to the case. I've got to find Apollo before Killjoy finds out he's missing. If I don't find him first, Mom will lose Lemontree Petting Zoo, and Apollo will probably be a goner. I shudder.

"Let's review the evidence while we wait." I motion for Crispy to follow me upstairs to my bedroom. As usual, it's littered with books, magazines, and various unusual rocks, crooked sticks, and weird rusted objects I've collected from my wanderings around our farm.

Crispy flops onto my bed and buries his head in my pillow.

I remove the tin can containing the evidence from its hiding place under my bed.

I take stuff out and hold it up, but Crispy doesn't look up from the pillow. Every now and then, he turns over and whimpers "Freddie!" and then covers his eyes with his arm.

I continue to hold up one item after another and act like Crispy is paying attention, even though he isn't. Maybe if I just keep talking, I can distract him from the pain of losing his best friend in the whole world. Crispy's suffering makes me glad my best friends are book characters. They aren't going anywhere.

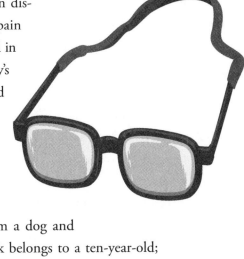

"So far, we know that the hair on the barrette is from a dog and not a human; the sock belongs to a ten-year-old; the pencil is probably Dad's; and the tug toy belongs to our ex-dog Zeus. The gold lapel pin in the shape of a curly letter M belongs to someone whose name begins with the letter M. That leaves those familiar eyeglasses, the leather glove, the coloring book page, and that weird green plastic thing." I glance over at Crispy. He has the pillow over his head. I exhale out loud and then continue with the evidence.

"The eyeglasses have a safety strap. So, either the wearer is active or prone to losing their glasses." I pass my magnifying glass over the strap and the glasses. "*Aha!* Another hair." That gets Crispy's attention. He sits up and tosses my pillow aside.

"This time, it's a brown hair." I use tweezers to free it from the hinge in the frame and carefully drop it into a baggie. "I'll have to examine it under the microscope to confirm that it's human. I doubt a dog would wear eyeglasses, but a detective never makes assumptions."

Crispy nods and wipes his nose on the back of his sleeve.

Now that I've got his attention, I don't want to lose him again. "Maybe the reason for the strap is to secure the glasses onto the head of an animal. Best leave open the question of *species* until I can get solid proof. I don't want to jump to conclusions. That kind of jumping can lead to bruised self-esteem when you're wrong."

I take off my own glasses and again try on the evidence glasses for size. They're very tight above my ears, so their owner must be younger or smaller than I am. When I look through them, my bedroom starts to spin. "The prescription is strong. The wearer cannot see without these glasses. So, it's weird they were found at the scene of the crime. Anyone with this kind of vision would have noticed them missing as soon as they lost them."

I write in my notebook: *The frames are purple with a green stripe down the arms. The hair is six inches long.* I put the glasses back into the Christmas cookie tin. As I do, I realize this will be our first Christmas without Dad.

I crawl up onto my bed and sit next to Crispy. It won't be the same without Dad. Nothing will ever be the same again. Dad's gone. Apollo's gone. Freddie's gone. The corners of my eyes start itching, and when I look into Crispy's swollen eyes, I almost burst into tears. I hold my breath, dig my nails into my palms, and promise myself I'm going to get them back. All of them. I'm going to find Apollo, free Freddie, and get Dad to come home.

If I win the Thompson Award, Dad will know I'm a doer and not just a dreamer. He'll come to the award ceremony. And when he sees Mom in real clothes—not her scrubs or overalls— he'll fall in love with her all over again. Mom is actually very pretty when she's not removing tumors or shoveling camel poop.

"When will Mom be out of surgery?" Crispy interrupts my daydream. "I'm worried about Freddie."

"Soon. Don't worry. We'll get Freddie back." I hold up the page from the coloring book. "Look at this. Whoever did this is not a conformist."

"You can tell from a coloring book if the person is flexible?" Crispy sits up on my bed.

I'm confused. Crispy must see it on my face.

"*Conformist.* That's someone who's very flexible, right?" He scoots to the edge of the bed. Now he's sitting right next to me. I ruffle his hair the way Mom does. His hair is coarse and damp from all his crying into my pillow. The musky scent of Freddie clings to him like the ghost of an old friend.

"You're thinking of *contortionist*," I say. "No, a *conformist* is someone who conforms, plays by the rules, colors inside the lines." I point to Dora la Exploradora's face. "The artist scribbled all over Dora's face instead of coloring it."

"Maybe she's just not a good colorer." He reaches for the page.

"That could be. But it doesn't look like she—or he—is even trying." I hold the paper out of his reach. "It looks like they're taking their frustrations out on poor Dora. Look how thick the crayon strokes are. They pressed down pretty hard on those Crayolas." I point to a blob of crayon wax on the paper. "I bet they broke their blue crayon, and this spot is where it snapped."

"Wow, you can tell all that from the scribbles on this page?" Crispy grins at me. "Can you tell whose it is? Who's the girl that lost it?"

"How do we know it's a girl?" I ask.

"Boys don't have Dora coloring books."

"How do you know?"

"Because I'm a boy." He jumps off my bed and picks up the green plastic thing.

"Well, not all boys are like you—thank goodness."

"What about this?" Crispy holds up the unidentified plastic thing.

"Yeah, what about that?" I take it away from him before he messes it up. I write in my journal: *Long green plastic thing covered with fabric. Elastic bands attached. Very dirty.* I pass my magnifying glass over it, and then I sniff it to confirm my hypothesis. "Grass stains."

"Can you tell whose it is?" Crispy asks.

"I don't even know *what* it is." It's bigger than the other evidence. I found it buried under the sawdust in a corner of Apollo's pen, like someone—or something—was trying to hide it.

"It's a shin guard, silly." Crispy laughs. "Soccer players wear them."

"Oh yeah, I knew that," I fib. "So, our suspect is a ten-year-old soccer player with a grudge against Dora la Exploradora, and her sidekick is a barrette-wearing dog," I say with a smirk. "Maybe it's a conspiracy and lots of people are involved. Or maybe these items aren't related and none of them have anything to do with the crime."

"And what about this?" Crispy holds up the glove. "It looks like a lady's glove."

"You're jumping to conclusions again." I take the glove and place it against the palm of my hand. "Definitely belongs to an adult."

"Whoever took Apollo plays soccer, wears ladies' gloves, and hates Dora la Exploradora," Crispy says, beaming.

"So it seems." I place all the evidence back in the cookie tin and put the lid on it. I push it back under my bed. "Now why would a girl who plays soccer, hates Dora, and puts barrettes in her dog's hair want to kidnap a cougar cub? We need a motive. If we can figure out *why* someone kidnapped Apollo, we can figure out *who* kidnapped Apollo."

"*Why* will tell us *who*," Crispy repeats.

"This evidence is the *what* that will tell us who, but only if we can figure out why."

"Whatever you say, Kass." Crispy shrugs. He pulls a folded piece of paper out of his shirt pocket and holds it out to me. "But if that stuff doesn't help us find Apollo, maybe this will."

10
THE FIRST RIDDLE

HOLY HIGH JINKS! **CRISPY HANDS ME** a typed ransom note, except it doesn't ask for any ransom. I read the note out loud: "I have four identical brothers. While they're running around town, I'm locked in the dark. But if one of them gets hurt, I come out to save the day. Find me and you find Apollo." I stare down at the black words on the white paper. "Where'd you get this?" I ask Crispy.

"I found it in Apollo's enclosure. Spittoon says it's a clue."

"Spittoon the camel?"

"Who else?"

"Did Spittoon say who left it?" I jump up and head downstairs.

"I didn't ask." Crispy is hot on my heels.

"Next time you talk to him, ask who left this note. Better yet, ask who kidnapped Apollo." Before Dad left, Crispy never heard animal voices.

I'm about to head outside when Mom appears in the doorway between the kitchen and her clinic. "The tech told me you lost Freddie. We'd better get a move on." Mom puts her coat on over her scrubs. "Animal Control closes soon. On the way, you two can tell me how Freddie ended up in Agent Pinkerton's van."

Still clutching the riddle, I slide into the passenger's seat of Mom's Jeep. *Four brothers . . . so he or she is the fifth child . . . unless they also have sisters.* I wonder if I should tell Mom about the note. She's so upset already, and I don't want her to get sick again. It's best not to stress her out.

After Dad left, the doctor said she had to avoid stressors. I think a ransom note counts as a big-time stressor. I've got to

find Apollo before Mom finds out he was actually stolen. Since she already reported the cub missing, Agent Killjoy is bound to find out very soon. Time is running out.

I let Crispy recount our adventure with Killjoy. Usually, I would correct his overblown descriptions and exaggerations, but at the moment, I'm too distracted by the ransom riddle. *Why would someone leave this clue? Why didn't they ask for a ransom? What do they want? And why did they kidnap Apollo?* My brain is on fire with questions.

Does this lion-napper even know what to feed a cub? Mom feeds him organic raw meat and green beans, which is why his coat is always so shiny and his teeth are so white. My heart sinks. I miss the little guy, even if he shredded my favorite hat and used my canopy bed as a scratching post. I've got to solve this riddle and find Apollo before he gets hurt . . . or worse.

"Kassandra Urania O'Roarke." Mom's voice interrupts my thoughts. "I told you to watch out for your little brother. You're almost a teenager; you should be more responsible." She shakes her head. "No television or electronics for a week. Both of you."

Crispy groans. That punishment will definitely affect him more than it does me. I still have my detective books and dictionary for entertainment.

Still, I can't help but defend myself. "If Freddie hadn't—"

"No excuses." Mom turns into the parking lot. "I'll deal with you both later. Now let's go get Freddie."

We arrive at Animal Control just before closing time. We rush into the empty lobby. The receptionist has giant eyeglasses perched on her beaky nose. With her mousy nest of hair and dull, squinty eyes, she looks like she could be Agent Killjoy's sister. *The* nameplate on her desk reads *Angelica Dworfman.* She has a whipped-cream mustache, crumbs down the front of her sweater, and a Starbucks cup in her hands.

"We're here to claim our hob," Mom says. "He weighs just under four pounds. He's sable colored with white socks."

"Hob?" Angelica Dworfman asks.

"A *hob* is a male ferret," Crispy says. "His name is Freddie."

The receptionist taps on her computer keyboard. "Let's see. I don't remember any ferrets coming in recently."

"You'd remember Freddie," I say.

"We don't get many ferrets." The receptionist flashes me a dull smile.

"Agent Killjoy took him," Crispy says.

Mom gives Crispy a chastising look. "What my son means is Agent Killjoy may have *found* Freddie."

"Where did you lose him?"

"The Pool and Splash park," Crispy says. "He slipped into the back of Agent Killjoy's van when we were—"

I kick Crispy in the shin before he tells the receptionist about our attempt to break into the Animal Control van.

"Ouch!" Crispy grimaces.

"The door was open, and Freddie went in after Agent Killjoy's dog biscuits," I say.

"Freddie loves dog biscuits," Crispy chimes in.

"It's true, Freddie can't resist a good dog biscuit," Mom confirms.

"Agent Killjoy hasn't returned from his rounds." Angelica Dworfman looks at her watch. "He's late."

"We'll wait." Crispy plops down on the floor next to the reception desk.

"We're about to close." The receptionist stands up and stares down at Crispy. "You can't sit there, young man."

"Ms. Dworfman, might you please just take a look and see if anyone has brought in a ferret?" Mom asks.

I join Crispy on the floor. A herd of dust bunnies swirls around us.

"We're officially closed." Angelica Dworfman hops up and comes around the desk. "Missy, mister, get up off that floor." She's not as small as her name would suggest. "You all have to leave now. If your ferret's here, you can claim him tomorrow."

Mom does a downward-facing dog and then sits cross-legged next to me. "We're not leaving until we retrieve our hob."

Even though Mom is mad at us, she's still got our backs. I smile at her, and she nods.

"Fine. Have it your way." The receptionist shakes her head and clucks her tongue. She sounds like one of the chickens Mom keeps behind the house.

The squealing of tires out front sends me to my feet. I look out the front window. "It's the yellow van."

"Let's get Freddie." Crispy springs to his feet and rushes past me.

"Wait for me," I say, running after him.

"And me!" Mom is out the door before I can catch up to Crispy.

The three of us descend on the yellow van. Agent Stinkerton Killjoy slams the door to the van and stomps around to the back. "I've got quite a haul tonight," he says to himself. When he chuckles, the hair on my arms stands on end. He reminds me of a mustachioed bad guy from a cartoon.

"Excuse me, Agent Pinkerton," Mom says in her nicest proper-lady voice.

Stinky Pinky looks over at her and his eyes go all goo-gooey.

"Margaret, it's good to see you." Pinkerton smiles. "It's been too long."

"Yes, it has." She fake smiles back at him. "Pinky, did you happen to find our missing hob—er, ferret?"

"Ferret? I haven't seen one of those in months. Excuse me." Stinky Pinky pushes past Mom and opens the back door of the van.

Crispy slides in between Stinkerton and the back of the van. "Where is he?" Crispy yells.

"It's okay, Skunk. We'll find Freddie." Mom takes Crispy's hand and starts to lead him away from the van.

"Wait, it's Freddie!" Crispy is jubilant. He's pointing at the back of the van and jumping up and down.

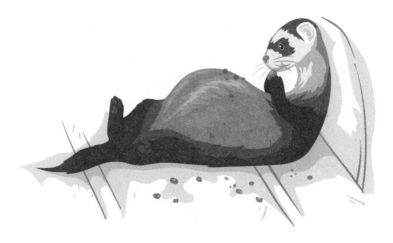

Slipping past Agent Stinkerton, I run over to see for myself. He must know he's outnumbered, because Killjoy stands back a few paces and watches us gaze into the cage inside his van.

Sure enough, there's Freddie, lying on his back, surrounded by biscuit crumbs. His belly's round and his eyes are glazed over.

"Food coma," Crispy says. "He ate too many dog biscuits." Crispy holds out his hand. "Freddie, come here, boy."

Drunk on dog biscuits, Freddie looks up at us, opens his mouth, and lets out a big belch.

"Freddie, for goodness' sake," Mom says. "Say *excuse me.*"

"Don't encourage him," I say. "Percy already thinks ferrets talk."

Mom turns back to Stinky Pinky. "Agent Pinkerton, may we take our bloated hob home now?"

"Do you have a permit for the rodent?"

"Actually, ferrets are domesticated polecats in the weasel family. They're not rodents," I say.

"Genus *Mustela*, species *M. putorius*," Mom adds. "And we don't need a permit." She isn't using her nice-lady voice anymore.

"Freddie's my best friend," Crispy blurts out.

Agent Killjoy laughs. "Silly boy."

Even though I agree, I still feel like punching Stinky Pinky right in the mustachioed kisser. *What a jerk!* "Give us our ferret and we'll leave." I try to sound tough, but my voice breaks. My hands are shaking, I'm so mad.

"That's enough, Pinkerton." Mom is definitely not using the nice-lady voice now. "Please don't talk to my son that way."

"Do you have any proof that you own this . . . ferret?" Agent Killjoy asks, holding the word *ferret* between his teeth like a dirty rag.

"Of course not," Mom says. "This is ridiculous."

"No proof, no rodent." Killjoy smiles. "Maybe we can discuss it over dinner, Margaret. Then I might forget that your juvenile delinquents were trying to break into my van this afternoon."

"Some things never change," Mom says. "You aren't blackmailing me into going out with you."

"Freddie's not a rodent!" Crispy yells. He kicks the back tire of the van, then runs past Killjoy and kicks the front tire.

Holy hubcaps! "That's it!" I catch up to Crispy. "You're a genius." I hug him. "I know how to find Apollo."

11

SPARE TIRE

WHEN WE GET HOME, CRISPY IS BESIDE HIMSELF. Freddie has to spend the night at Animal Control. Mom promises she'll get him out tomorrow.

After Mom heads inside the house, I pull Crispy to the rear of Mom's Jeep. I point at the spare tire mounted on the back.

"Spare tire. That's the answer to the riddle." I smile at Crispy. "I figured it out when you kicked Killjoy's tires."

He just nods and stares down at his tennis shoe.

I run my hands around the spare tire. "Four identical brothers running around town. The fifth brother in the dark until one of the others gets hurt." But what does a spare tire have to do with Apollo? We aren't going to find our cougar cub inside this spare tire. Is there anything to find here? I pull my handy pocket-sized flashlight from my spy vest and examine the tire.

"Look," Crispy says, pointing at something small and white poking out of the tire cover.

I pull on the corner and out comes another note. The same as the first, it has black letters typed on white paper.

"We're lucky it didn't blow away while we were driving to Animal Control." I hand my flashlight to Crispy. "Hold the light." I read the note out loud. "Two legs I have, and this will confound, for only at rest do they touch the ground. Find me and you find Apollo." I look over and Crispy is grinning.

Clever boy. He must know the answer. "Do you know the answer?" I ask.

"You're the detective, not me." Crispy hands me my flashlight. "I'll ask Spittoon and Chewy. Maybe one of them knows the answer."

"So the camel and the chimp are experts at riddles?" I shake my head. "More like *vittles*. They eat their weight in food every day."

"Dinner's ready." Mom's voice startles me. She's standing in the doorway, waving a big spoon. "Come inside and wash up."

I tuck the riddle into a pocket of my spy vest and head inside.

I wonder where she's hidden the vegetables tonight. She's an expert at sneaking kale or zucchini in where they don't belong. Looks like chili, rice, salad, and corn bread. My stomach growls. You really work up an appetite chasing dogcatchers and solving riddles . . . not to mention searching for your missing cougar cub, wondering when your mom will rescue your brother's ferret, worrying you'll lose your petting zoo, and worrying that you'll never see your dad again.

I sit down at the table and stare into my chili. I'm moving kidney beans around with my spoon, looking for telltale green specks. It looks like real chili. It smells like real chili. I scoop up a spoonful, blow on it, then taste it. It's still hot and burns my tongue. After it cools off and my tongue quits hurting, I dig in, enjoying the spicy warmth on my tongue. It's actually pretty yummy.

"This had better not be meat." Crispy holds up his spoon. "You know I don't eat meat."

"It's textured vegetable protein." Mom smiles. "It's not meat. I know you're a vegetarian, Skunk."

"Textured what?" I drop my spoon. I told you she sneaks in vegetables where they don't belong. I examine a piece of corn bread. Yup—sure enough, green flecks. "What's in this bread?" I ask.

"Try it. It's good," Mom says with a wink.

I nibble on the corner of a piece of corn bread. Knowing Mom, there probably isn't even any corn in this bread. It's probably made from air, spinach, and some mysterious sea vegetable. The texture's like cat litter.

"Yummy," I say, wishing I could spit it out. I quickly eat my chili, avoiding the rest of the corn bread. "May I be excused?" I'm hoping my praise and good-faith attempt to swallow a bite of spinach bread will put me in Mom's good graces. "I have homework."

"Don't you want some dessert? I made chocolate zucchini cake."

It couldn't have been less appetizing if she said she'd made the cake with used hay from the petting zoo. "Maybe as a reward for finishing my homework." I don't tell her I'd actually rather eat my homework than her vegetable cake.

"Percy, want me to help you with your homework?" I ask, trying to lure him out of the kitchen.

"After I have some cake." My brother's munching away on cat litter bread, scarfing down textured vegetable protein, and looking forward to cake made out of a green gourd.

I exhale loudly and head for the front door. I'll have to solve the riddle on my own and leave him to his fake cake.

Sitting on the porch, admiring the Big Dipper in a cloudless sky, I'm thinking about the riddle. *What has legs that only*

touch the ground when it's resting? The riddle itself is not the only clue here. The fact that someone is leaving riddles is also a clue. Who would do that and why? Why has someone sent us on this wild-goose chase to find Apollo? Or should I say *wild-lion chase?*

I unfold the paper. It could have been printed on any printer anywhere. But someone planted this piece of paper on our Jeep. Someone was here, returning to the scene of the crime. That suggests the culprit lives nearby or has transportation, a bicycle or a car. It seems unlikely that the kidnapper could have carried Apollo on a bike, so they must have a car—or an Animal Control van. But Stinkerton would never leave notes like this. He's not that clever. And our mountain lion–napper is very clever.

But who could it be? And how do the riddles and the other evidence fit together? Is Crispy right? Is the kidnapper a soccer-playing, Dora-hating, riddle-loving ten-year-old? Does her leather glove–wearing mother (whose name starts with *M*) drive her to our house every day to leave clues? I shake my head. There's just too much evidence, and it doesn't fit together.

"Are you working on your story?" My brother's voice surprises me.

"What story?"

"The story for the school newspaper so you can win that prize."

"I've got to find Apollo and catch the kidnapper, then I'll worry about my story." I can't believe he's thinking about my story when Freddie's still at Animal Control and Apollo is who knows where. I twist my hair into a ponytail, wrap it in a bun, and stick a pencil through to hold it up. Getting the hair out of my face might help me think. "If the kidnapper would only strike again, I could follow their trail."

"You want another kidnapping?"

"I'm speaking hypothetically, for the sake of the investigation." I refold the riddle and put it into a pocket of my spy vest. "Are we the only targets of this kidnapper? Or are other animals disappearing?"

Mom pokes her head out the door. "I thought you were doing your homework."

"I'm thinking." I purse my lips. Thinking is work, too.

"Feed the animals and then come inside. It's getting chilly." Mom disappears back into the house.

Crispy and I head to the petting zoo for the evening feeding. Monkey chow and a banana for Chewy, gluten-free dog food and an apple for Raider, and pig pellets and half a cabbage for Poseidon. I use the pitchfork to fill the wheelbarrow with hay, and Crispy delivers it to Spittoon. He comes back with the wheelbarrow, and I refill it. Then he lifts the wheelbarrow and heads out toward the pasture to feed Morpheus.

"Wait! I've got it." I race after Crispy. "Two legs have I; only at rest do they touch the ground." I look down at the wheelbarrow. It has one wheel in front and two legs behind that must be lifted to make it move. "The wheelbarrow's legs only touch the ground when it's at rest."

Sure enough, there's a folded piece of paper tucked between the leg and body of the wheelbarrow. I slide the paper out and unfold it. It's another riddle with the same black type on the same white paper. I push my glasses up my nose and read it out loud. "*I run constantly, but I never walk. I have a mouth but never talk. I have a bed but never rest. I have a bank but don't invest. Find me and find Apollo.*"

12

SHRIMP FAUX PAWS

CRISPY AND I ARE RIDING THE CITY BUS into downtown Nashville to visit Dad for the weekend. I wish we could just stay home and search for Apollo. The ten-minute bus ride seems to take forever. But Mom says riding the bus will give us independence and build character. *Whatever.*

I'm frustrated with all these riddles and clues. The case just isn't coming together like it should. Even worse, we don't know if poor little Apollo is okay. And then there's Freddie. Animal Control still won't release him. Agent Stinkerton Killjoy insists ferrets are a public health hazard. The only thing hazardous about Freddie is his odor. Mom might have to make Dad sue Animal Control to get him back.

The good news is the last riddle I found, the one stuck to the wheelbarrow, was super easy to figure out. The bad news is I'm still no closer to finding Apollo. I pull the piece of paper from my spy vest pocket and reread it. "*I run constantly, but I never walk. I have a mouth but never talk. I have a bed but never rest. I have a bank but don't invest. Find me and find Apollo.*"

"Did you figure it out?" Crispy asks.

"A river." I refold the paper and stick it back in my vest. "The riddle is easy, but what river and where? How can we search every river in Tennessee, or even in Lemontree Heights, for that matter?"

"Spittoon thinks the lion-napper didn't go far. He feels it in his hump."

"Spittoon's hump intuition?" I offer Crispy one of the chocolates Butler gave me at school yesterday. "We have a lot of clues but not a lot of leads. The camel's hump might be our best bet at this point."

"Maybe Dad can help." Crispy's eyes light up. He still thinks Dad is one of us. I'm not so sure.

Speak of the deviled egg, Dad and Zeus are waiting for us at the bus stop. Dad must have come straight from work. He's still wearing a suit and tie, and his auburn hair is slicked back. His green eyes sparkle when he spots us. I wave at him, and he waves back.

"Dad!" Crispy jumps up, scrambles off the bus, and runs right for Dad.

"Whoa there, buddy." Dad laughs and picks him up like a little baby. *How embarrassing.* "How about a hug?" Dad says to me.

I blow at my bangs. What can I do? I just hope he doesn't try to pick me up! The familiar citrus smell of his aftershave almost makes me cry. "When are you coming home?" The words spill out. "I mean, when are you coming to visit Raider and Spittoon? They miss you."

"They do?" Dad squeezes me so tightly I can hardly breathe. "I miss them too, kiddo." The scissors in my spy vest poke me in the ribs, but that's not the only reason there's a pain in my chest. My heart hurts from missing him so much. The telltale itching invades the corners of my eyes, and I close them tightly. I don't want to let go.

Zeus's tail is whacking my legs. Crispy drops to his knees and puts his arms around the dog's neck. "You've got to help us get Freddie back." Crispy stands up and grabs Dad's hand. "And Apollo too."

"Slow down, sport." Dad glances over at me. "What happened to Freddie and Apollo?"

While we walk from the bus stop to Dad's town house, Crispy tells him about Agent Killjoy capturing Freddie and how Apollo's been missing for three days. Dad just nods. I suspect he thinks Crispy's just telling whoppers. I try to get a word in, but Crispy is talking a mile a minute. I give up and follow behind them until we reach Dad's apartment.

Dad's girlfriend, Mari, opens the door, holding a plate of fresh-baked coconut cookies. It's totally no fair because I love coconut. *Holy honey cake!* Those cookies smell so good. My stomach growls, and I put my hand on my belly to shut it up.

"No, thanks. I'm not hungry," I fib. I won't give in to Mari's temptations, no matter how hungry I get. Her bribery won't work on me. I'd gladly eat Mom's gluten-free veggie cakes for the rest of my life if Dad would just come back home.

Crispy grabs a cookie and stuffs it in his traitorous little mouth. I scowl at him. Mom would be furious if she knew Crispy was eating cookies before lunch. They probably aren't even gluten-free. My mouth waters, but I don't give in.

"Veronica's watching a movie in the den." Mari points toward a room just off the entryway. "I'll call you when lunch is ready."

I didn't come here to visit Ronny. I came to visit Dad. Why am I here if all we're going to do is watch TV? I could be continuing my investigation and searching for Apollo. This trip is such a waste of time. I scoot past Mari and head for the den.

What Mari calls the *den* is really just Rotten Ronny's playroom. It's equipped with all the latest technology, including a fancy computer and a bunch of electronic games. Ronny is totally spoiled. All she does is play games, watch TV, and eat delicious homemade goodies.

"Hi, guys." Ronny is sitting cross-legged on the floor, munching on cookies and watching *Dora la Exploradora* on an elephant-sized flat-screen TV. This Dora is older than I remember her being. She has a group of new friends, along with her monkey (Boots) and Swiper the fox.

"Wait. Dora looks older," I say.

"This is *Dora and Friends*. She's ten now," Ronny says. "Same age I am." She points to a bowl of Kit Kats on the coffee table.

As usual, Crispy stuffs a couple in his pocket. Sometimes Mom searches his pockets when we come home and confiscates his smuggled candy bars. Like a pack rat, he has a stash of Kit Kats in his bedroom closet.

On screen, a cute brown-haired boy flashes his perfect white teeth. "Is that her boyfriend?" I ask. I don't remember him from the original cartoon.

"That's Pablo, and he's just a friend." Ronny glares at me. With her short hair, big eyes, and baggie shorts, she looks exactly like Pablo, Dora's "just friend." Except Ronny wears glasses and is a girl.

"Where's Freddie?" she asks.

"Don't ask," I say.

"He's in prison at Animal Control." Crispy pouts.

"Mom is getting him back right now," I say, hoping it's true.

I plop down in an overstuffed chair. Even though I'm too old for cartoons, to be polite, I watch Dora and her friends navigate the rain forest to rescue Map and Backpack, who've been stolen from Boots by Swiper.

Whenever she hears the whisking sound of Swiper about to swipe something, Yara, Ronny's shih tzu puppy, barks at the screen. The puppy is wearing a pink ribbon in a tuft of black hair standing straight up on her furry little noggin. Who puts ribbons in their dog's hair? Probably the same people who put barrettes in their dog's hair. That's as bad as Crispy putting clothes on a chimp.

A lightbulb goes off in my head. A black-and-white dog who wears ribbons might sometimes wear barrettes. Could Crispy be right about the barrette I found belonging to Ronny? I glance at Rotten Ronny and wonder . . .

Crispy picks up a soccer ball from the coffee table. "Is this new?"

"Yeah, Daddy got it for me."

What? Rotten Ronny calls *my* father *Daddy?* I feel like snapping that elastic band attached to her glasses and slingshotting her eyeballs across the room.

Crispy drops the ball to the floor and kicks it toward Ronny. "We're not supposed to play soccer in the house." She kicks it back. "Hey. Quiet, guys. This is my favorite part."

Swiper is trying to steal strawberries out of Backpack but gets tangled in his own spring-loaded swiping device. Ronny is laughing her head off, and Yara is barking her head off.

"Does Swiper steal from Dora because he wants her stuff or because he wants to annoy her?" I ask.

"Sometimes he returns what he takes," Crispy says. "He's more sneaky than bad."

"I like Swiper," Ronny says. "For him, stealing stuff is a game."

We're in the middle of a hot debate about Swiper's motives when Dad and Zeus appear at the door. "Wash up. Time for lunch."

I pat my spy vest and remember Dad's pencil. Stalling for time before I have to face Mari again, I say, "I found this in the petting zoo." I take the mechanical pencil from one of my pockets and hand it to him.

"Hey, I've been looking for that. I wonder how it got out there." Dad looks from Ronny to Crispy and back to me.

"Don't look at me!" Ronny is lying on the floor, balancing her soccer ball on one foot. The puppy is jumping up her leg and barking at the ball, her topknot wagging as fast as her tail.

"Lunch is ready!" Mari shouts from the dining room.

"Come on, guys, wash your hands." Dad leads the way to the bathroom and reminds us how it's done by singing a full chorus of "Happy Birthday" while lathering his hands long enough to kill all the germs. I know it's stupid, but it makes me miss him even more. We take turns washing and singing and then head into the dining room.

The food smells amazing—the sticky perfume of jasmine rice, the savory scent of stewed black beans, and the sweet smell of ripe plantains. Plantains are giant Caribbean bananas. Mari is Cuban and cooks lots of yummy Cuban food I try my best not to like. My mouth waters as I sit down at the table.

The table settings look good enough to eat: green ceramic plates on top of purple place mats. I must be hungry if I want to eat my place setting. Everything's perfect.

Whenever I visit Dad, I'm afraid to touch anything because the place is so nice. Unlike our house, it doesn't look lived in. It looks like one of those magazine houses. Mostly, I'm afraid if I break something, Dad won't like me anymore. When he lived with us, I never thought about whether or not he liked me. He was just my dad. Now, I'm on pins and needles whenever I'm around him. It's weird. It's like he's a different person or something, except he isn't. I don't even know how to explain it.

Mari fills our plates with rice, beans, plantains, and shrimp. *Holy herbivore!* This will be interesting. I hold my breath when she passes a plate to Crispy.

"What's that?" Crispy points at the shrimp. He's been a vegetarian ever since he was four and learned that meat came from animals. He refuses to eat his animal friends.

"It's *camarones*," Mari says.

Crispy stares at his plate. "Is *camaroni* an animal or pasta?"

Mari looks at Dad with hurt in her eyes. "I thought he didn't eat *carne*."

Dad shrugs. "I didn't realize meat included shellfish."

"*Camarones* are shrimp," Ronny says. "Do you eat fish?"

I'm enjoying this. Usually, Crispy scarfs down everything Mari cooks. Now she's done it. Crispy will never trust her again, trying to make him eat his animal friends.

"Fish are animals," Crispy says. "I don't eat anything with a backbone."

"What about jellyfish?" I ask. "Would you eat them? They don't have backbones."

"How about slugs?" Ronny chimes in.

Crispy wrinkles his nose. "Correction. I don't eat anything that moves." He pushes his plate into the center of the table.

"It's my fault," Dad says.

"You eat bacteria and fungus," I say. "And they move."

"Gross." Ronny scrunches up her face.

"If you eat cheese and mushrooms, then you eat bacteria and fungus too."

"I don't eat fungus!" Rotten Ronny waves her fork in the air. "Like Swiper, I eat strawberries."

With a wilted expression, Mari picks up Crispy's plate and takes it to the sink. She brings him a new plate without the shrimp. "I'm so sorry. Next time, I'll make a nice meal without any creatures. So sorry."

Mari looks like she's about to cry. She tries hard to make us like her, but I resist her sweet and savory bribes. And now all the points she got with Crispy for those homemade cookies have been canceled out by the shrimp faux pas. In English class, we learned *faux pas* means *false step* in French. I imagine shrimp taking false steps with their tiny faux paws.

13
FIRST SUSPECT

ALL WEEKEND, I TRY TO FIGHT OFF a niggling suspicion. It doesn't make sense, but I can't shake it. I take a deep breath to clear my head. Let's review the facts:

Rotten Ronny is a ten-year-old girl who wears glasses attached to her head with an elastic band. She plays soccer and wears dirty white socks. She has a mom with a name that starts with the letter *M*. She's got a black-and-white dog that wears pink ribbons and probably wears pink barrettes too. To top it off, Ronny loves Swiper the fox, who is a thief, which isn't the same thing as hating Dora la Exploradora—so I might have been wrong about the meaning of the scribbles on the coloring book. Maybe she's just a crummy colorer. But is Ronny clever enough to have written the riddles?

I watch from the balcony as Crispy and Ronny kick the soccer ball around in the courtyard. Crispy tramples over a flower bed while chasing the ball. I'm surprised they don't get in trouble for playing in the courtyard. It's very fancy with brand-new landscaping and benches around the edges and a fountain in the middle.

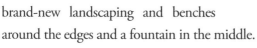

Ronny skirts the edge of the lawn, dribbling the ball with her feet like a pro. She's wearing one green shin guard and one blue one. Now I see why she has an elastic band holding her eyeglasses in place. She's a terror with a soccer ball. If it didn't look so dorky, I might consider getting an elastic band for my glasses. That way, they'd stay on my head when the mean boys throw me up against the lockers at school, and I wouldn't have to keep pushing them back up my nose when they slide down.

Ronny zips past Crispy, dribbling the ball with her feet. Those mismatched shin guards are a dead giveaway. She must be the lion-napper. All the clues point to Ronny. But why—and how—would Ronny swipe Apollo? And where would she put him if she did? I've got to get more conclusive proof that the stuff left at the crime scene belongs to Ronny to know for sure. I can't just go accusing her of stealing—that is, unless I never want to see Dad again. If I accuse Ronny of kidnapping Apollo, that will be the straw that breaks the camel's back for sure.

I have to prove Ronny kidnapped Apollo. If I can get a strand of her hair, I can compare it to the hair from the eyeglasses frame I found at the scene of the crime. But how am I going to get one of her hairs? As much as I'd like to, I can't just run out into the courtyard and yank one out.

I've got to find her hairbrush—if she uses one, which is doubtful by the looks of her unkempt hair. I go back inside. Holding on to the banister, I tiptoe up the stairs to the second floor. I'm about to open the door to Ronny's room when I hear Mari coming down the hall, her princess heels tapping on the wooden floor.

I duck into the hall bathroom and shut the door. I don't see any signs of Ronny in this bathroom. The fancy granite double vanity is spotless, and everything in here belongs to adults, stuff like shaving cream and mouthwash.

Since I'm here, I slowly pull open the top drawer of the cabinet looking for a hairbrush. I find a jumble of toothpicks and dental floss and spare toothbrushes. I continue with the second drawer. Interesting . . . on the outside, the place is perfect, but open a drawer and things are a mess.

Aha! A brush filled with brown hair. I examine it more closely. Strands of red hair are mixed in. It could be Mari's or even Dad's. Judging by the bling-bling hair clips keeping it company, and the majority of brown hairs, I assume the brush must belong to Mari—unless Dad has a double life. These days, I wouldn't know. These days, he's more like a stranger than my dad.

I pull a couple of strands from the brush and secure them in a baggie. Like I said, I always carry baggies in my spy vest.

You never know when you might have to collect a sample or store a clue.

Since this brush clearly isn't Ronny's, I still need to sneak into her bedroom and snatch some hair. I listen at the door. I can barely make out Dad's voice coming from the hall. Dad and Mari are whispering.

"They wouldn't do that," he says.

"Every time they visit, things go missing."

Whoa. Is Mari accusing us of stealing?

"It's probably that ferret," Dad says.

I feel like bursting out of this bathroom and telling her we aren't the thieves. Her own daughter, precious little Veronica, is the thief and a kidnapper to boot!

But where would Ronny hide a cougar cub? Is there a river nearby? Apollo's not in this town house; if he were, we'd hear him. Apollo is not the shy, quiet type. He'd rip this place to shreds. I almost wish he were here. I smile imagining Mari's precious floral drapes and throw pillows ripped to shreds. I'm not any closer to finding Apollo. But I just might be closer to catching his kidnapper.

I listen at the door again. I don't hear anything. Dad and Mari must be gone. I open the bathroom door a crack and peek out. The coast is clear. I make a break for it and dash into Ronny's bedroom and close the door. *Whew.* I lean up against the door to catch my breath.

Ronny's room looks like it could be a centerfold for *Youth Soccer Magazine.* Her trophies are neatly arranged on a shelf. Her wall is covered with posters from the US women's soccer team. Her favorite player seems to be someone named Hope Solo. It sounds like a name from *Star Wars.*

To my surprise, Ronny is extremely neat. Everything is in its place, which comes in handy for detective work. I open the top drawer of her dresser. Her underwear is folded and stacked according to color. I peek under one stack—nothing but a soccer-themed drawer liner. In her closet, soccer uniforms hang in a row like a starting lineup ready for the playoffs. Below, her cleats and sneakers dangle in matched pairs from a shoe rack.

I kneel in front of her bookcase and remove each book in its turn: *The Secret of the Old Clock*, one of my favorite Nancy Drew mysteries, something called *For Soccer-Crazy Girls Only* about Alex Morgan. Judging by the cover, it's another book about soccer.

Hey, what's this? I spot a *Dora la Exploradora* coloring book crammed in the back of the bookcase. I pull it out. This confirms my suspicion. Ronny is a terrible artist. And sure enough, it's missing a page. Evidence! I stuff the coloring book inside my vest.

I head for the bathroom. Yeah, Rotten Ronny has her own bathroom. I told you she's spoiled. Inside, her toothbrush and toothpaste lean inside a glass with—you guessed it—Hope Solo's picture on it. I spot a dark shadow inside the glass. I pick it up. A comb! *Now I've got you.*

I lift the comb from the glass and examine it for stray hairs.

"Hey, what are you doing in my room?" Ronny shouts.

Shrimp and grits! I didn't hear her come in. I quickly drop the comb in my pocket and turn around.

"Mom!" Ronny shouts at the top of her lungs. "Kassandra's rummaging around in my room!"

Yara starts barking her head off.

"Your room is so neat," I say. "Great picture of Hope Solo." I try to distract her. "Is she related to Han Solo?"

"Mom!"

Yara won't stop yapping.

"What's all this racket?" Mari appears in the doorway with Dad close behind her. Yara stops barking and starts growling at me.

"Kassy's going through my stuff." Ronny pulls on the front of my spy vest, and the Dora coloring book falls out onto the floor.

"I told you she's a thief," Ronny says with a smirk while Yara nips at my ankles.

Shih tzu puppy! I'm busted.

14
THE RIVER OF NO RETURN

THE LAST FEW HOURS AT DAD'S TOWN HOUSE are an interrogation. They might as well have put me under a bright light and scratched a chalkboard. I told them I was investigating Apollo's kidnapping, but they didn't believe me. Dad just shook his head with that disappointed look on his face that makes me want to crawl in a hole. I wish he'd punish me or yell or something, but he just keeps shaking his head and tightening his lips. Now he'll never want to come back.

I try to tell him I'm sorry, but the words won't come out. Instead, I choke back tears.

Eventually, Dad drives us home, but the tension in the car is suffocating. I think I might throw up. I don't know why, but he promises not to tell Mom, at least for now. When he pulls up in front of the house, he just watches me getting out of the car, still shaking his head, disappointment dripping from his eyes.

"Bye, Dad," I whisper as I climb out of the back seat. "I'm sorry."

"See you next week," Crispy says.

"Be good," Dad says. "And don't stress your mom."

I hang my head and slink into the house. I've never been so glad to be back home in my life. At least Mom's still on my side.

Mom is lining up jars of formaldehyde on the kitchen counter. I don't want to know what those hideous blobs floating inside are. No doubt some experiment she's doing for the good of animal kind. If Mari's kitchen belongs in a *Home Beautiful* magazine, ours belongs in a zoology textbook.

"How was your visit to your dad's?" she asks.

I drop into a chair, lean my elbows on the breakfast table, and put my chin in my hands. "I don't want to talk about it." At least at home, I don't have to be careful not to scratch the floor or dent the cabinets. They're so full of chips and gouges, no one would notice another nick. Our old farmhouse is the opposite of Dad's sparkling new town house.

Mom sits next to me at the table. "Cheer up. Look who's home." She points to a box in a corner, where a ball of fur is curled up on one of my brother's old sweaters.

"Freddie!" Crispy slides across the kitchen floor and scoops up his best friend. You can guess how Freddie shows his affection. "You got him back!"

"How'd you spring Flatulent Freddie?" I ask.

"Don't call him that." Crispy cuddles the ferret. "He can't help it. Can you, buddy?" He kisses Freddie between his beady little eyes.

"Flatulence is healthy and natural," Mom says. "It's good to pass gas."

"So, when someone lets go a stinker, we should congratulate them?" I go to the cupboard, take out some peanut butter, and grab a spoon.

Mom gets up and wraps Crispy and Freddie in a group hug.

"Mom, stop." Crispy wriggles free. "You'll squish Freddie."

I take my peanut butter and spoon back to the table. "How did you convince Agent Stinkerton to hand over Freddie?" I ask, peanut butter sticking to the roof of my mouth.

"Kassandra Urania." Mom glares at me.

"What?" I ask with a mouth full of peanut butter.

"Don't eat out of the jar. Why don't you make a sandwich?" Crispy grabs the jar away from me.

"Hey!" I say, but it's too late. I settle for licking the spoon.

"Freddie and I will make sandwiches."

"Don't let Freddie touch my sandwich." I watch Freddie helping himself to peanut butter straight out of the jar using his grubby little paws. I wait for Mom to scold Crispy, but she

doesn't. *So, the ferret can eat right out of the jar, but I can't?* That doesn't seem fair.

"Animal Control hasn't found Apollo yet." Mom looks worried. "I asked about him when I picked up Freddie."

"But what if Agent Killjoy captures poor little Apollo?" My question is more like a protest, and Mom frowns at me.

"At this point, I don't care who finds him just as long as he's okay," Mom says. She sounds exhausted. Between the vet clinic, the petting zoo, and us, she doesn't get much rest.

"I care who finds him," I say. Apollo won't be okay if Animal Control finds him. I've got to find him first.

"You'll find him," Crispy says to me, jabbing the air with a peanut butter–covered knife. "You'll write about it and win that newspaper prize."

Freddie is on the counter helping himself to the loaf of bread. At least he's not drinking out of Mom's formaldehyde jars.

"Mom, are there any rivers around here?" I'm thinking of the last riddle: *I run constantly, but I never walk. I have a mouth but never talk. I have a bed but never rest. I have a bank but don't invest.*

"There's the creek that runs along the old property. Why?"

"So maybe it's not a river but a creek." I jump up from the table. "Creek works too."

"What do you mean? Where are you going?" Mom asks. "Your brother was kind enough to make us sandwiches. Please sit down and show some gratitude."

I exhale loudly. *What can I do?* I sit down and wait for Crispy's wonderful sandwiches. I'll do my duty and eat one, but then I've got to get down to that creek.

Mom smiles as Crispy sets a plate of messy sandwiches on the table. She picks one off the top of the stack and takes a bite. "Delicious. Thanks, Skunk."

"Why do you call him Skunk?" I ask to distract her. I can barely sit still I'm so eager to go search for Apollo.

Mom laughs. "When he was a baby, he was worse than Freddie."

I mouth *Ha-ha-ha* at my brother, grab a sandwich, and take a bite. It's actually pretty good for gluten-free bread, sugar-free peanut butter, and all-natural apricot jam.

"Don't listen to them." Crispy tears off a crust and holds it out for Freddie. I eat my sandwich as fast as I can.

"What's gotten into you?" Mom asks. "What's your rush?"

"There's something I have to do before it gets dark."

"I don't want you near that creek." Mom's look bores a hole into my skull. "Do you hear me? It's not our property anymore."

"Yes, Mom." I cross my fingers behind my back.

"And wipe the jam off your face." Mom hands me a napkin.

I dutifully wipe my face. I even clean up the dishes. I've got to stay on Mom's good side, especially after what happened at Dad's.

"Do you want to play soccer in the backyard?" I ask Crispy.

He narrows his eyes. "You don't play sports."

"You can teach me."

He narrows his eyes at me, clearly suspicious, but follows me outside anyway.

When I step outside onto the porch, the scent of the flowering bushes framing the front of the porch hits me like a sweet sucker punch to the nose. The porch runs along the front of our house, and from it we have a view of the barn and the animals when they're outside. There's a storm brewing tonight, so the animals are all inside the barn. Well, all except poor little Apollo.

Once we're out of Mom's earshot, I say, "Come on, we're going to the creek."

"Mom said not to go to the creek." Crispy sits there gulping like a frog.

"Do you want to find Apollo or not?" I grab him by the shoulders and look him straight in his frog face. "The note says find the creek and we find Apollo."

Crispy wriggles free and takes off toward the petting zoo.

"Hey, where are you going? The creek's this way." I point to a stand of trees to the right of the house.

Crispy ignores me, so I race after him. I catch up to him at the barn. He grabs a halter from a hook and a carrot from the cooler, then heads past the barn and out toward the back pasture.

Dark clouds are forming overhead, and lightning cracks across the sky. *Deep-fried catfish!* The storm is almost here. A raindrop hits my face. My brain tells me we should go back inside the house; my heart tells me to go to the creek. It's up to me to save Apollo and the petting zoo and keep Mom from getting too stressed.

I've almost caught up to Crispy. "What are you doing?" I shout as I run. The grass is damp and slippery. I'm going as fast as I can without falling down.

Crispy stops at the wooden fence. "I'm getting Spittoon." He whistles, and the camel comes running across the pasture. "He'll help us find Apollo."

"We can't take Spittoon to the creek." *What's going on in my brother's little frog brain?* "Mom doesn't want *us* down there. She'll croak if she finds out you took the camel." The wind is whipping the halter around in Crispy's hands. The sky is spitting rain, making dark spots on my jean jacket.

"Apollo is Spittoon's best friend." Crispy slides the halter around the camel's head and leads him through the gate. "Plus, he knows where Apollo's hidden."

15

THE SHED

I'M SPRINTING ACROSS THE PASTURE, trying to keep up with Spittoon. A bolt of lightning and a crash of thunder make me jump. Crispy is riding the camel, straddling his back just behind the hump, and Freddie is riding Crispy. The fierce headwind is making it hard to keep up with them, and my hair blowing in my face doesn't help. To make matters worse, it will be dark soon. Maybe going down to the creek isn't such a good idea.

We reach the edge of our property and enter the woods. Branches are whipping around in the wind. I'm out of breath but keep running anyway. Roots and shrubs keep trying to trip me. I stumble a few times but catch myself before I fall. As fast as I go, I still can't keep up with the camel.

Spittoon lumbers down an incline and stops at the creek bed. Crispy jerks the reins to the right. The camel takes his time responding, but then they're off again.

By the time I reach the creek, Spittoon is already climbing up the bank, heading toward Mr. and Mrs. Busybody's house. I lean over and put my hands on my knees, trying to catch my breath. The howling wind is giving me the creeps. It sounds like something out of a horror film.

A dark shadow falls on the creek, and I glance overhead. Black clouds roar with thunder, and lightning cracks across the sky. We'd better hurry and find Apollo so we can get back home before this storm gets any worse. *Kale chips!* Another clap of thunder makes my heart leap. Even the ground is shaking from the rumbling storm.

"Crispy, wait up!" *Run faster, run faster*, I tell myself. "Guys, wait for me."

I shouldn't have opened my mouth because now it's full of hair. Distracted by my hair, I trip over a branch. "Ouch!" My shin hurts. I pull up the leg of my jeans. My shin is bleeding. No time to bandage it now. I've got to catch up to Crispy. *Where in the world is he going?*

I get to my hands and knees, take a big breath, and launch myself into action. I sprint as hard as I can, panting and sweating. My clothes are sticking to my body. And even though I'm sopping wet, I'm hot from running so much. The rain actually feels good on my face. I open my mouth to take in a few drops of water. I'm dying of thirst.

Too bad I can't go ten days without water like a camel. Spittoon can go over a week without drinking and drink over fifty gallons in three minutes. But whatever Crispy says, camels can't talk. And he isn't a detective who can lead us to our missing cougar cub. So why am I running after him?

The rain goes from spitting to spraying. Wet hair slaps me in the face as I run. My spy vest protects my torso from getting soaked like the rest of me, but my tools are slamming against my chest with every step, like someone is punching me in the ribs.

Spittoon and Crispy are up ahead. They've stopped near an old shed, where Dad used to keep the riding lawn mower. I'm closing in on them. When I catch up, Spittoon is in the middle of a sneezing fit.

"Where in the dell are you going?" I ask, out of breath.

Crispy dismounts and leads Spittoon to the door of the shed. "Spittoon says Apollo's in here."

I stare at my brother in disbelief. Here we go again. True, the shed is near the creek, and the creek is the answer to the riddle. Could Spittoon really smell Apollo in there? As if he can hear my thoughts, the camel sneezes again.

The door to the shed is banging in the wind. Crispy dashes inside. When Spittoon follows him in, his sneezing gets worse.

Maybe Apollo is inside, and that's why the camel's allergies are acting up.

I scramble into the shed after them. "Apollo?"

The shed is empty except for a rusty bucket, an old sawhorse, and some dilapidated shelves falling off the wall. Oh, and lots and lots of cobwebs. Something crunches beneath my boot. I'm afraid to look down. "Hey, what's this?" Bits of kibble are scattered around the floor, and a chewed-up plastic water bowl is pushed into a corner.

Spittoon nudges the water bowl with his snout and then bursts into another round of sneezing. As I'm wiping camel snot off my sleeve, I notice a piece of paper tacked to one of the shelves. I rip it down.

Not another riddle, I hope. I unfold the white paper, and sure enough, the same black type is printed in the center of the page. I read out loud: "*What king can you make if you take the head of a lamb, the middle of a pig, the flank of a buffalo, and the tail of a dragon?*"

"He's supposed to be here!" Crispy's face is so white that he looks like he has the head of a lamb. "Why isn't he here?"

"Calm down and help me solve this riddle." I stare down at the paper, but it's hard to concentrate with the wind howling and the thunder clapping. "*The head of a lamb, the head of a lamb.* What does that mean?"

"We've got to find him!" Crispy shouts.

"What do you think we're trying to do?" I glance over at my brother. I hope he's not going to be sick. He doesn't look so good. "*The head of a lamb, the middle of a pig, the flank of a buffalo, and the tail of a dragon,*" I repeat.

"Lion! Lion! Lion!" Crispy yells. "The head of a lamb is *L*, the middle of pig is *I*, the flank of a buffalo is *O*, and the tail of a dragon is *N*. That makes *L-I-O-N*: *lion.*" Is my brother trembling? He's sopping wet. He must be cold.

"Very clever! Okay, so where's our lion?"

"I don't know!" Crispy screams.

"Well, he isn't here. Our kidnapper has led us on another wild-lion chase." I glance around the shed. "Judging by the teeth holes in that water bowl, he's been here." I pick a tuft of gold hair out of a crack in the floor. "And given Spittoon's cat allergy and nonstop sneezing, it couldn't have been that long ago." I examine the hair. It's Apollo's, all right. I drop it into a baggie so I can confirm my hypothesis under the microscope at school. "We've got to find him!" Crispy is distraught.

"Isn't that what we've been trying to do for the last few days?" My brother goes all this time as happy as a farting ferret in a wagonful of dog biscuits and only now freaks out that Apollo is missing? What's his problem?

Holy heartbreak! He's crying. I grab him by the shoulders. "Don't worry. We'll find him." I try to sound more certain than I am. "We know he was here, and I don't think he's been gone long. You and Spittoon look around the shed. I'm going to gather more evidence."

"I was just trying to help," Crispy sniffles.

"I know. You're a big help." I pull him into a hug. *Aargh.* The ferret licks my nose. "Spittoon led you here because he knew Apollo was down here. Maybe he can track the cub. But you'd better hurry while his scent is fresh."

A clap of thunder makes me jump again. "The storm's getting worse, and it's almost dark. Maybe we'd better head home and continue the search tomorrow."

"But what if something's happened to Apollo?" Crispy whines.

I take a tissue from my pocket and hand it to him. "Judging by Spittoon's allergic reaction, the cub was here within the last hour. And he's had food and water, so he's okay." I point to the kibble and hand Crispy another tissue. "You and Spittoon check around the shed and then head home." No need for both of us to get grounded for staying out past dark.

"What about you?" Crispy blows his nose and hands the tissue back. *Brothers are gross.*

Holding the Kleenex between my thumb and forefinger, I drop it into a baggie—not because it's evidence, just to get rid of it. "I'll be right behind you. Now go." I push him out the door. "Get Spittoon home before you both catch nasty colds."

Crispy nods and leads the camel back out into the storm.

16
THE STORM

RUMBLING THUNDER SCARES ME, and I accidently drop my magnifying glass into the slimy water bowl. I lift it out by the handle and wipe the lens off on my jeans. I have to stay calm, gather evidence, look for clues, and then get the heck out of here and go home.

Okay. *Concentrate.* First, judging from Spittoon's allergic reaction, Apollo was here not long ago. Then there's the food and water. The fact that the kibble is strewn across the floor means someone was eating it, someone who eats off the floor.

Another roar of thunder and flash of lightning reminds me the storm is getting closer. Mom will have piglets if I'm not home soon. She's probably worried sick. Maybe I should have told her about the riddles, but I didn't want to add to her stress by telling her Apollo was kidnapped. I exhale out loud. Her only daughter missing during a possible tornado is probably a major stressor. But what can I do now? I've got to gather the evidence while it's fresh. All good detectives know that clues go stale if you wait too long.

The wind whips the shed door shut, and I'm standing in the pitch dark. *Holy hair-raising thunder!* Maybe I wasn't exaggerating about that tornado. I'd better hurry and finish my investigation and get home.

I pull my mini-flashlight from my pocket and quickly scan the floor. *What's with all the half-eaten bat wings on the floor?* I aim the beam at a dark object in the corner. *Aha!* Lion scat. There has definitely been a lion in this shed. *How many lions are wandering around Lemontree Heights?* It has to be Apollo.

Biscuits and gravy! Something touches my hair. *Was that a bat?* I hate bats! My scalp itches just thinking about those flying rats. Actually, bats are not rodents. They belong to the family *Chiroptera*, not *Rodentia*. Rodents or not, *I've got to wrap up and get out of here before they attack.*

I shine the light around the dank shed, looking for more clues. Another tuft of yellow hair attached to a board catches my eye. I yank the hair loose with my tweezers and drop it into a baggie. Apollo was probably rubbing up against the two-by-four. Either that or our kidnapper has golden hair and likes to rub their head against posts.

On closer inspection, I notice scratches on the wood. Someone's been clawing at it . . . someone with very sharp claws. Spittoon was right. Apollo was certainly here. But who brought him to this shed and why?

I examine the floor with my wet magnifying glass and see faint paw prints in the dust. Each kidney-shaped pad is topped with four teardrop toes. Luckily, one of my first picture books was about how to identify animal scat and tracks, so I know my paw prints.

The kidnapper's footprints must be here too. On hands and knees, I crawl around, trying not to smear any of the possible prints. I'm glad I have wipes in my spy vest because this place is disgusting. The smell of bat guano is enough to make me hurl. I bury my nose in my sleeve and continue my search one-handed.

Tiny dots in the dust must be mouse prints. With my magnifying glass, I can make out what looks like tiny versions of the cougar cub print, only with rounder toes spread further apart. A mouse has four toes on each of its front feet and five toes on each of its hind feet. These are bigger tracks. A rat maybe? *Cringe.* I hate bats, but I don't love rats either.

Wait! These prints have an extra pad mark. *Aha!* They have five toes with claws, a main pad shaped like a frowning mouth, and a distinctive back toe. Plus, the thumbprint is at an angle, not like mouse or lion prints. *Yup!* They're ferret prints, all right.

They must be prints from when Freddie jumped down to snack on some kibble. *No wonder he's getting so fat.* I smile to myself.

The sole of my shoe has a diamond-shaped shoe print pattern and matches some of the freshest footprints. Then there are smaller shoeprints with a zigzag pattern. They must be Crispy's. That's it. No more shoe prints. It's odd the kidnapper didn't leave any prints. The dust is thick and damp, almost mud. Anyone who stepped into this shed would certainly leave footprints. So, who else has come in here besides me, Crispy, Apollo, and Freddie?

Another clap of thunder reminds me I'd better conclude my investigation and head home before Mom has a conniption. The wind is so strong it's pelting the side of the shed with loose branches. My skin prickles every time I hear the snap of a bough. This storm is a doozy. I'm going to get drenched on my way back.

When I stand up, a glint of silver catches my eye. I pick up a Kit Kat wrapper from a low, dusty shelf. Apollo is a kit-cat, but he doesn't eat Kit Kats. Whoever brought him here must have dropped it—a litterbug and a kidnapper. I seal the evidence in a baggie. I think of the bowl of Kit Kats at Dad's town house. Ronny's favorite candy.

Yup. All clues point to Ronny: the eyeglasses, the soccer shin guard, the Dora coloring book, and the stinky sock at the crime scene; and now a Kit Kat wrapper at the hideout. I should have confronted Ronny and Mari when I had the chance. Of course, that would have meant the end of my relationship with Dad, what's left of it.

But why would Ronny kidnap Apollo? And how? She doesn't have a motive or the means. And how could she have left those riddles? Something just doesn't add up.

Boom! Crash! Suddenly, I'm sitting on my bottom on the dirty floor. My glasses flew off my head on impact. *Holy hurricane!* What the heck just happened? Was it an earthquake? It sounded like an explosion.

I crawl around on the sticky floor, feeling for my glasses. It's dark in the shed, and without my glasses, I'm blind as a bat. *Oh, why did I have to think about bats?* I hit my head against a post. *Ouch!* A crash of thunder makes my heart skip a beat. *Where are my glasses?* I'm officially freaking out. It's like the end of the world outside, and inside I'm being sucked into a vortex of bats. I put my hand to my face to wipe off a tear, but then I remember how disgustingly dirty my hand must be and change my mind. I pound the floor with my fist. *Wait!* I feel something under my palm. *My glasses!*

I slide my glasses on and wait for my eyes to adjust. I can see shadows now— mostly shadows of bats circling above my head. *Aaak!*

I'm afraid to look outside. I stand up, brush off my jeans, and tiptoe to the door. I don't know why I'm tiptoeing. Maybe because the shed is swarming with angry bats who didn't like the earthquake either. With my arms flailing to keep them away from my face, I dive for the door to escape.

The door won't budge. I push with all my might and only manage to crack it open half an inch. *Rice and beans!* A giant tree has fallen in front of the door. I'm trapped in here with a swarm of bloodthirsty bats. *Holy hazard! Now what?*

I wish I'd asked Crispy to wait for me. He and Spittoon are probably home by now, enjoying kale chips and gluten-free cupcakes. My stomach grumbles. I consider the kibble crunching under my boots. It probably tastes about the same as Mom's homemade health cookies.

A pair of bats swoop at my head. "Aaaaaahhh!" I scream. My arms are whirling like a propeller to keep the nasty things from getting stuck in my hair or biting my face. I take a deep breath and remind myself these are not vampire bats. They are regular brown bats and prefer snacking on mosquitoes to drinking human blood. The mosquitoes are the bloodthirsty beasts I should be worried about, especially since I'm allergic to their venom. When they bite me, I get welts that swell and blister. Not pretty.

I smack a mosquito lunching on my bare arm, and warm blood oozes out of its body. I fight back tears and remind myself that detectives, spies, and reporters don't cry.

I'm going to die here, face down in bat guano and eaten by giant mosquitoes. When they find my rigid body, it will be covered in swollen red blotches, and my last meal will have been dog kibble and the emergency granola bar from my spy vest. I don't care if spies, detectives, and journalists don't cry. I can't help it. I wipe a torrent of tears off my cheeks with the back of my hands.

17

FATE

DO YOU BELIEVE IN FATE? How about a more practical question: do you know how to take a door off its hinges? I've tried every tool in my spy kit, along with the clip on my barrette and the buckle of my boot. I check my vest again: baggies, magnifying glass, tiny scissors, Dad's old Swiss Army knife, tape, string, paper clips, fingerprint powder, my notebook and pen, and my emergency granola bar. Amazingly, none of these things help me escape this shed and get back home before dark.

If Crispy doesn't come back for me soon, I'm going to meet the same fate as my namesake, only instead of a cage, I'm going to die in this dusty old shed. I wonder if the mythical Kassandra had bats circling her head before she died.

I only hope Crispy and Spittoon found Apollo and made it safely back home. Then at least I won't die in vain. Eventually, Crispy will have to tell Mom where I am. Until then, I might as well gather facts just in case I live.

Holding the flashlight in my mouth again, I remove the last riddle from my pocket and examine it with my magnifying glass. *Holy hummus!* A chocolate thumbprint. I hold my thumb up to it to compare. The kidnapper's thumb is smaller than mine. Now I've got hard evidence. The Kit Kat–eating kidnapper finally left her signature.

Taking advantage of the last of my flashlight battery, I scan the shed again for any other clues I might have missed. There are dusty old paint cans on one of the shelves. Otherwise, they are bare except for massive cobwebs. A fat spider with crooked legs is guarding the largest web. I back away so as not to disturb her.

Something catches on the toe of my boot. I shine the light on it. *What the . . .?* It's the lilac underpants from one of my American Girl dolls. I used to play with dolls, but now they just sit on a shelf in

my room.
That must
be why I didn't
notice anyone was
missing her underpants.

Even before I exam-
ine the underpants, I know.
Yup! Ferret scat. I stuff the stinky
briefs into a baggie. *Aha!* Now it all
makes sense.

Holy hoodlum! My brain feels like it
will explode. I know who kidnapped Apollo!
And if I make it out of here alive, I'm going to
throttle him.

That's why Freddie was the only one not wearing
underpants at the birthday party. Those dirty undies are the
smoking gun I've been looking for! Finally, all those crazy clues
fall into place.

I'd wondered why Crispy wasn't more upset when we
discovered Apollo missing. Thinking back, he seemed almost
happy. Instead of crying, he grinned and said I'd have my big
scoop for the newspaper. He only started bawling when we got
here and the shed was empty.

Crispy must have expected to find Apollo here and got
scared when we didn't. He knew Apollo would be in this
shed because he's the one who put him here. My harebrained
brother has been hiding the cub in this shed for the last four
days. I can't believe it. And I can't believe no one noticed Crispy
sneaking out to bring food and water to Apollo.

He almost had me fooled. I was starting to think Spittoon really did know where Apollo was hiding. Spittoon's not a bloodhound after all. Crispy led him here to cover his own kidnapping tracks. And I fell for it.

I sit cross-legged on the damp floor and let that sink in. Crispy planned this whole thing, the wild-lion chase with those silly riddles and then the charade of Spittoon leading us here. *But why? Why did he do it?*

It dawns on me that Crispy planted all the evidence I found at the crime scene—except maybe his own button and the half-eaten licorice. He probably just dropped those while pulling off this crazy caper. But why is he framing Ronny? The barrette, the Dora picture, the sock, and the shin guard are all hers.

No wonder Dad thinks I'm a thief. Crispy's been stealing Ronny's stuff from Dad's in order to frame her for the kidnapping. He's been very clever but not clever enough to outsmart me.

My stomach growls. Absentmindedly, I pull the emergency granola bar from my pocket. Munching distracts my stomach so my brain can get back to work.

Jeez. Crispy must have been stealing things from Dad's for a while. He's going to be in big trouble when Dad finds out.

Now I know *who*, but *why*? Why did he do it? Crispy had the means, but what was his motive? Why would Crispy kidnap his own lion? And why would he frame Ronny? Crispy actually likes her. I'm the one who's jealous and wishes she'd be abducted by aliens. At least, I think he likes her. Then it dawns on me. Maybe he likes her *a lot* and that's why he's framing her. Maybe he has a crush on her. Is that why he took her stuff? But why hide Apollo? It still doesn't make sense. None of it makes sense.

Mrs. Cheever says to be a good reporter, you have to be courageous and follow a story all the way to the truth, even if at first it doesn't make sense. Of course, that's what got me into this mess in the first place—that and my pesky little brother.

Yes, the world needs to know the truth. I open my notebook and put my mini pen to paper. *To whoever finds my body, this is the story of how my little brother, Perseus Charon "Crispy" O'Roarke, is responsible for my death.*

18
THE MOTIVE

THIS IS ALL CRISPY'S FAULT. Not just my being trapped in this stinky shed but everything. It all started when Crispy burned down the hay barn. Then Dad left, and Crispy started hearing animal voices and stealing stuff, and now I'm going to die in this abandoned old shed.

Sometimes I dream the barn is still standing, the horses are back in the pasture, and I'm skipping stones on the pond. Then I wake up, and by the time the morning dew washes the sleep from my eyes, I'm shoveling pig poop and wiping camel snot off my school clothes.

I hear a growling noise and hold my breath. *Wait.* It's just my stomach again. I look at my wristwatch compass—standard spy issue. It's almost five in the evening. No wonder my stomach is growling. Except for one granola bar, I haven't eaten anything since my bowl of gluten-free cereal for breakfast. *Holy hankering! I'm hungry.* I finger the last emergency granola bar in my pocket. Being locked in a shed definitely counts as an emergency. But I need to ration my rations. I may be here awhile.

The temperature is dropping fast, and I hug myself to keep warm. My fingers are numb, and my eyes sting. But detectives, spies, and reporters don't cry. I sniffle and wipe my nose on the sleeve of my jean jacket.

A weird thought flashes through my mind. *Ridiculous. No way.* My little brother's not that weird, is he? I'm still trying to figure out his motive. Could it be that he did it for me? *Was he dumb enough to kidnap Apollo so I'd have my scoop?* I shake my head. What a nutso idea. Come to think of it, he seemed more concerned about my story than I was. And he kept bringing it up. He kept saying, "Now you have your story," and talking about the newspaper.

It's all so confusing. My head is spinning. I need sustenance to nourish my brain cells. I chew the last bite of my granola bar as long as I can before swallowing it. I glance at the kibble and half-eaten bat wings strewn across the floor. *Nah.* I'm not that hungry. But I am thirsty.

Luckily, I always carry a small flask of water in my vest. I unscrew the top and take a sip. Rationing my water is more important that rationing my food. A human can go weeks without food but only days without water. I've got to get out of here before I run out of water. I'm trying hard not to panic. A good detective, spy, or reporter never panics.

Flashlight in my mouth again, I examine the rusted hinges. My trusty Swiss Army knife has a screwdriver. I align the screwdriver with the screw and then lean against it with all my might. I can't get the rusted screw to budge. The harder I try to twist, the more the screwdriver strips the threads on the screw.

The door is so old and rotten—maybe I can pry it off its hinges. I switch from the screwdriver to the knife blade and wedge it between the hinge and the door. When the blade starts to bend, I stop. I remove the buckle from my boot and wedge it into the crack I've made. The crack widens a teeny-tiny bit, but the door is still firmly attached.

Another bat swoops down at me. When I wave it away, I notice a tiny sliver of light coming from the ceiling, where the bats are going in and out of the shed. If they can get out through the roof, maybe I can too.

The shed is on the edge of Mr. and Mrs. Busybody's property (which, as you know, used to be ours). If I can attach the flashlight to my pointer and get the light through the hole in the roof, maybe someone will see it.

Dad gave me this pointer; it's a cool retractable metal rod that looks like an old-school car antenna. It can telescope out to three feet long and then collapse again to fit in my pocket. He says no one uses pointers anymore because of computers. If I can rig up a beacon using my pointer and flashlight, maybe I'll be rescued. Of course, then I'll be stuck here in complete darkness with those nasty bats.

I push all thoughts of flying non-rodents from my mind and busy myself rigging up my makeshift beacon. I tape the flashlight to the retractable pointer, extend it as far as it will go, and eye the dusty, old shelves. Maybe I can use the shelves as a ladder to reach the roof. Luckily, the shed is small and the roof is low.

With the rod between my teeth, I climb up on the sawhorse, grab the highest shelf with both hands, and do a chin-up. I'm dangling a few feet off the floor, face-to-face with a big, hairy spider. I hiss at the spider, and she scurries away. Maybe I'm weird, but spiders don't bother me.

I pull myself up far enough to slide my right elbow onto the shelf. Holding on with one hand, I use the other to grab the flashlight from my mouth. The weight of my dangling body nearly makes my arm slip off the shelf.

Aiming a flashlight attached to a metal pole at a tiny bat hole in the dark while dangling from a flimsy shelf is no easy feat. I keep trying for and missing the hole. My arm is getting so tired that I don't know if I can hold on. And the tape around the flashlight is starting to loosen. If I don't get the rod through the roof soon, the flashlight will fall off and so will I.

I take a big breath and then, with all my might, I jam the flashlight through the bat hole. *Bingo!*

BAM! *Ouch!* Hitting the floor knocks the wind out of me. I sit gasping, looking up at the pointer hanging from the roof. My glasses fell off again, and all I can see is a dim spot of light. I must have managed to get the flashlight through the hole and somehow it stuck. Hopefully, the battery will hold out long enough for someone to see the beam and find me. If not, I'll be spending a very scary night in this bat-infested shack.

19
THE ENCOUNTER

AT LEAST THE STORM STOPPED. A ray of moonlight pierces the roof. I find my glasses. I must have landed on top of them. The frames are bent and both lenses are cracked. It's no use wearing them. Anyway, what's there to see in here except bats?

Luckily, before I sacrificed my flashlight and busted my glasses, I finished writing the whole story for whoever finds my body. Then Percy Charon "Crispy" O'Roarke will have some explaining to do. It's his fault I'm trapped in this shed and won't make it to my thirteenth birthday. I'll die never having owned a cell phone.

A rustling noise outside makes me perk up my ears. "Help!" I drop my notebook and jump up. "I'm trapped in here! Help!" I shout at the top of my lungs.

The sound of twigs snapping and leaves rustling gets closer. I bang on the door and yell as loud as I can: "Help me! Please, help me!"

A gruff voice shouts back, "Do you have the lion in there?"

"What?" I ask, confused.

"Are you hiding him?" the scary voice asks.

"It was my brother—"

"Stay there," the voice interrupts.

Duh. Like I'm going anywhere. "Okay?" It comes out as a question.

I listen as the footfalls recede into the night. "Wait! Come back! Help me!" I scream. "Don't leave me here!"

I balance my cracked glasses on my nose. I can sort of make out the numbers on my glow-in-the-dark spy compass watch. It's five thirty. I can't believe I've been trapped for almost two hours. At least now someone knows I'm here.

But who? He didn't sound very nice. Maybe I'm safer in here with the bats than being rescued by some random man wandering the woods. And why did he ask about Apollo? Who else knows Apollo is missing? Was it Mr. Busybody? It didn't sound like him. He has a high, tinny voice, not a deep, threatening one.

Mom must have had those piglets by now. *Please, Crispy, spill the beans and tell her where I am.* Knowing him, he's fibbing so he doesn't get me in trouble. Apparently, he's been coming down to the forbidden creek every day to feed Apollo, not to mention stealing a bunch of stuff from Dad's apartment. *Wow.* My little brother is a lion-napper and a thief. How could he do this to Apollo? To me? To Mom?

I guess that explains the half-eaten bats on the floor. Who knows? Maybe Apollo was having the time of his life in here chasing bats. He obviously *loves* them.

I unzip a baggie, remove the Kit Kat wrapper, and lick the chocolate off it to keep my strength up. I savor the last drop of water from my flask and eye the slimy water bowl on the floor. If worse comes to worst, I'll have to make myself drink that sludge to survive.

"Help!" I yell. "Are you coming back?" I listen in darkness. Nothing but the creepy sounds of nighttime.

Why would Crispy do this to me? Why would he hide Apollo in this shed and pretend the cub was kidnapped, even going to the trouble of leaving those ridiculous riddles?

Suddenly, a terrifying idea creeps into my brain, one I should have thought of before. *If Crispy brought Apollo here and kept him in this shed, where is the cub now?* Did he get out, or did someone steal him? I think back to when we got here. The door was open. So, either Apollo wandered out or someone took him. *Oh no!* Maybe Stinkerton captured him and he's shutting down the petting zoo at this very moment.

Or what if Apollo wandered out and got hurt? I'm trying to remember if cougar cubs have any natural predators in Tennessee. He's still pretty small. An eagle or a hawk might be able to pick him up. I shudder.

Keep calm. Concentrate. Use your brain, I tell myself. *Think.*

Okay. The cub has been missing from the shed for less than twenty-four hours or Crispy would have fessed up. He seemed shocked Apollo wasn't here. And he must have been coming out here at least once a day to check on the cub. So, it's reasonable

to assume
Apollo either
escaped or was
captured earlier today.
But where is he now?
Yikes. Holy hubbub! A loud
buzzing gives me a start. My brood-
ing must have distracted me, because I
didn't hear anyone approaching. But there's
definitely someone right outside the door with a
chain saw, sawing the tree trunk, hopefully to set me
free. Finally. Thank goodness.

I plug my ears and peek out the door crack. Through the
cracks in my glasses, I make out a couple of men in the moonlight, both wearing hats. One is fat and the other is skinny. The
skinny one is manning the chain saw while the fat one watches.
The fat one looks familiar. I squint and try to recognize him.

Shiitake mushroom! It's Agent Stinkerton Killjoy of
Animal Control.

ZO

MR. AND MRS. BUSYBODY

MY HEART IS RACING. I hide in the shadows and wait to confront the evil Agent Killjoy. If he knows about Apollo, we're sunk. Mom will have to close the petting zoo, and we'll lose our animals. Crispy will never recover. And neither will I.

And if Killjoy's already found Apollo, then all is truly lost. I've failed as a detective. Maybe Dad's right and I'm just a dreamer. "Earth to Kassy." My eyes are burning. Why did I ever think I could find Apollo and save the petting zoo?

The door opens, and I'm face-to-face with Mr. Busybody and Agent Killjoy. In the moonlight, with his pointy snout and glowing eyes, Killjoy looks just like a vampire bat. No wonder I hate bats.

"Kassandra, are you okay?" Mr. Busybody asks. His eyes look clouded over, the way old people's do.

"Where's the lion?" Killjoy blusters into the shed. His fat head swivels as he scans the room. "Where are you hiding him?"

Despite Killjoy's booming voice and threatening glare, I'm relieved. If he's asking about Apollo, that means he hasn't caught him yet. Hopefully, Crispy found him, and our adventurous cub is safely tucked into his enclosure back home.

"I'd better call your mother." Mr. Busybody taps his cell phone with his bony fingers.

If I had a phone, I wouldn't be facing my nemesis at this very moment. I could have called for help and been home reading the dictionary by now. I could have called Mom to come and get me. Then she would have called Dad. And they would be working together to rescue their only daughter. "Earth to Kassy."

I hate to think of what will happen to me when Mom finds out I disobeyed a direct order and came down to the creek. Still, I'd rather be grounded for life than stuck in this disgusting shed for another minute.

I get a whiff of musk, and a familiar ferret winds between Killjoy's legs and scurries toward me.

"Freddie!" He stands on his hind legs and paws at my shin. When I bend down and pick him up, my messed-up glasses fall off again. I pick them up, along with Freddie. I'm so glad to see him, I kiss his little black nose. "Wait. What are you doing here?" It dawns on me that Freddie on the loose means trouble. *Where's Crispy?*

What happened to Crispy? Didn't he and Spittoon go home? My stomach flips as I consider the alternatives. Maybe he fell into a ravine, or got hit by lightning, or tripped over a tree root and broke his leg.

"Where's Crispy?" I ask Freddie as if he could answer.

"Not that rodent again." Killjoy laughs. In this light, his teeth look like razors.

I tighten my grip on the ferret and lean back just in time to evade Agent Stinkerton Killjoy's giant paws as he tries to grab Freddie.

"Leave us alone!"

"If I left you alone, you'd still be trapped." He's so close I can smell his foul breath.

When Killjoy takes a step closer, I move backward and my heel catches the edge of the water bowl. It flips over, clanging. The slimy water splashes on my ankles. I stumble but catch myself before Freddie and I end up on the filthy floor.

"Lucky for you, when I was searching for that lion, I saw a light coming from the roof." Killjoy's mustache twitches when he talks.

"I saw the lion rolling in my catnip," Mr. Busybody says. "Freaked me out, so I called Animal Control."

"By the time I got here, the blasted thing was gone." Killjoy shakes his crooked finger at me. "I bet you know where he is."

Killjoy's beady glare makes my stomach flip again. It's not easy facing your nemesis on an empty stomach. I must be starving, because right about now, I'd trade my spy vest for a piece of Mom's chocolate zucchini cake.

"I've been stuck in here. I don't have any idea where Apollo is."

"That sounds right to me." Mr. Busybody flashes a crooked smile. "We'd better get you home. Your mother's worried sick.

I promised to bring you back." He gestures at Agent Killjoy. "Come on, Pinkerton. You can look for the lion tomorrow."

Your mother's worried sick. The words haunt me.

"I'm going to find your lion and shut down Lemontree Petting Zoo." Killjoy is so close now I feel his hot breath on my face. "I've already filed an injunction to get the place shut down. What kind of operation loses a dangerous lion?" He shakes his head. "Your petting zoo is a safety hazard. Your mother knows better."

I feel like someone punched me in the stomach. I can't breathe. *An injunction to get us shut down. Oh no!*

"Apollo is just a cub. He wouldn't hurt anyone," I say as I squeeze past Killjoy and scoot outside.

It's dark and damp outside, but after the storm, the air is sweet. I hug Freddie to my chest and try not to cry. I should be happy to have escaped, but I'm worried about Mom and Apollo and Crispy and Lemontree Petting Zoo. My whole life—what's left of it—is collapsing.

"Come along," Mr. Busybody puts his hand on my shoulder.

"Thanks for getting me out," I say. "Have you seen my brother, Percy?" At the sound of my brother's name, Freddie squeaks.

"No, I haven't." He gestures toward his house. "Come on. Let's get you inside for a cup of warm cocoa, and then I'll drive you home. Your mom's worried sick."

Worried sick. The words echo through my head. If Mom gets sick again, it will be my fault.

The lights of Mr. Busybody's house in the distance are a welcome sight for once. He leads the way, even though I know this land like it was my own—because, well, it used to be. Agent Stinkerton follows us, grumbling under his foul breath.

A few yards from the shed, Freddie slips out of my arms and disappears into the darkness. "Freddie," I call into the night. Crispy will hate me if I let anything happen to his best friend. Although, after what Crispy did, I don't know why I care.

Agent Killjoy pushes past me and chases the ferret into the woods. I hear a scream, then a thud, and then cursing in Killjoy's booming baritone. He must have tripped over a stump and fallen on his face. Serves him right.

Leaves rustle behind me, and I spin around. Freddie is back, only now he's riding on Crispy's shoulders. The clever ferret led Killjoy in circles.

"Crispy! What are you doing here?"

"I came to find you."

"Does Mom know you're here?"

"No. I snuck out." Crispy looks me up and down. "What happened to you?"

"I almost died in that shed because of you." I narrow my eyes at my little brother. "Why did you kidnap Apollo and hide him out here?"

"Kassandra?" Mr. Busybody calls out. He must be hard of hearing, because he doesn't even turn around, not even after the ruckus Killjoy made. He's all the way to his back door before he notices I'm not behind him. He's standing on his porch under the floodlight, blinking one eye at a time like a tortoise.

"I'm here, Mr. Busselberg," I answer. Yeah, his name isn't really *Mr. Busybody.*

"Come get some hot cocoa, and then I'll take you kids home." He shields his eyes with his hand and peers in my direction. "Sarah made a cherry pie. I'll call your mom again and ask if it's okay if you have some pie before I drive you home." He taps on his phone again.

My stomach growls. Hot chocolate and pie sound so good. Will I be a traitor if I take food from the Busybodies after they stole our property? Well, they didn't actually steal it, but you know what I mean.

"Pie and cocoa." Crispy looks up at me with hungry eyes. Freddie chirps.

"Since it's dark, we'd better let Mr. Busybody take us home. And then you've got a lot of explaining to do." I grab the sleeve of Crispy's jacket and pull. "Come on. Let's get inside before Agent Killjoy catches up to us. He'd love nothing more than to recapture Freddie . . . well, except for catching Apollo."

21

GROUNDED

MOM IS WAITING AT THE FRONT DOOR when we get home. She doesn't look happy. She has her hands on her hips. That's never a good sign. As I step up onto the porch, I notice her eyes look puffy like she's been crying.

"We almost found Apollo," I say in my own defense. "He was trapped in that old shed down by the creek." I'm tempted to spill the beans about Crispy, but he looks so pathetic I feel sorry for him.

"I don't want to hear your excuses." Mom has tears in her eyes. "I told you not to go down there."

The tears must be contagious, because my eyes sprout them too. "It's my fault—"

"You're both grounded for a month and no TV or Internet," Mom interrupts. "Homework and school, that's it." She wipes her eyes with the back of her hands. "Wash up and go to bed now. It's way past your bedtime."

"How are we going to search for Apollo if we're grounded?" My voice cracks.

"You're not." Mom points to the stairs. "Pinkerton will find him. Now go to bed."

"No!" Crispy sniffles.

"Not Animal Control," I burst out. Mom's frown warns me not to say anything more.

"Upstairs. Now!" Mom never yells. *Holy hornet!* She must really be angry. "Tomorrow after school, you'll clean the petting zoo until it shines."

Crispy and I race each other up the stairs.

"You'd better be in bed when I get up there!" Mom's voice trails us upstairs.

"This is all your fault," I say to Crispy when we reach the landing. "Why? Why did you do it?"

"I wanted to help you get your big scoop."

"What?"

"You said you needed something to happen. A crime, like kidnapping or theft."

"You're kidding me."

"I was just trying to help," Crispy pleads. "I never meant for Apollo to escape."

"Yeah, well, he did, and now he's lost for real." I shake my head. "And now we're grounded and Killjoy will capture him. You've ruined everything!" I slam my bedroom door in Crispy's scrunched-up face.

I go through the motions of washing my face, brushing my teeth, and getting ready for bed. After hours in that dirty shed, I really need a bath, but I'm just too exhausted to do anything but plop onto my bed and stare at the ceiling. I'm even too tired to read the dictionary.

My story for the *Cub Reporter* is a bust. Dad thinks I'm a thief. Mom is furious. And Crispy . . . well, I'm not speaking to him. He's the one who got me into this mess. At least he's got Freddie for company. Who do I have now that I've alienated my entire family? What a disaster.

After Dad left, I thought things couldn't get any worse. I was wrong. Now, even Mom is mad at me. Poor little Apollo is out there somewhere, fending for himself with the evil Stinkerton Killjoy hot on his trail. I'm grounded. How can I rescue Apollo when I'm stuck at home? Worst of all, we might lose the petting zoo. Then where will we be? Mom could have another nervous breakdown, and Dad will never come back. Percy and I will be orphans.

A knock at my door signals my doom. Has Mom come up to say good night or to scold me? Guess I'm about to find out. She enters without waiting for me to say "enter." I thought I'd trained her to knock before barging in.

Mom lets out a big, disappointed sigh and then sits on the edge of my bed. "What happened tonight?" When she gazes down at me with questioning eyes, I look away, embarrassed.

A cricket scurries across the floor. I imagine I'm a baby cricket, and it's my mother, and I follow it into a hole in the wall. "Well?"

I look up, and Mom is still waiting for an answer. I guess she didn't come to say good night. She came to interrogate me.

"Apollo was stuck in that old shed by the creek. I had proof he was there. But by the time we got there, he was gone." I put my pillow over my face.

"No need to be so dramatic." Mom lifts my pillow off my face and strokes my hair. "How'd you know he was there?"

"I followed the riddles to the creek, and then Spittoon started sneezing." As I say it, I realize how ridiculous it sounds. Somehow, I still can't bring myself to rat out Crispy, the little fiend.

"What riddles?"

"We found some riddles." I point to the pile of dirty clothes draped across the chair. "They're all in my vest."

"Why didn't you tell me about these?" Mom slides the papers from my pocket and unfolds one. She reads it and then looks at me, eyes wide with surprise. "Who left these?"

Biscuits and gravy! A direct question. "I'm not at liberty to say." (I learned that on television.)

"Kassandra Urania O'Roarke. You'd better tell me and quick."

Apparently, the line worked a lot better on TV. Some things just don't translate well into real life.

"Mom, you've got to let me look for Apollo." I sit up and hug my pillow to my chest. "Please." Tears sprout in my eyes.

"Pinkerton assured me he would find him," she says.

"That's what I'm worried about!" I pound my fist into my pillow. "If he finds Apollo, he'll get us closed down." I'm sobbing now. I know detectives, spies, and reporters don't cry, but I can't help it.

"Kassandra, stop crying. You're being unreasonable." Mom reaches for my hair, but I jerk my head away. "Pinkerton talks big, he always has. But he's a softy at heart."

Has she gone off the deep end? Agent Stinkerton Killjoy, a softy? *Yeah, and I'm a six-foot purple gorilla.*

"But he wants to close us down." I fling myself back onto the bed. "Agent Killjoy's out to get us."

"Pinky is still hurt because twenty years ago I went to prom with your dad instead of him." The corners of Mom's mouth turn up just a little bit, and she has a weird look in her eyes.

"You didn't go out with Stink—I mean Agent Killjoy?" *Please say no.* The thought of the evil Stinkerton and Mom makes me want to puke.

"He wasn't Agent Killjoy back then, just a guy with a crush."

The twinkle in Mom's eye worries me. She doesn't actually *like* Stinky, does she?

Holy horror! What if Mom marries him and the evil Stinkerton Killjoy becomes my stepdad? I think I'm going to be sick. I bury my face in my pillow and don't say another word. Not even when Mom says, "We'll finish this conversation in the morning. Good night, Petunia."

22
INTERVIEWING THE NEIGHBORS

THE NEXT MORNING, MOM WAVES THE RIDDLES under my nose at breakfast. She demands I tell her who left them. I pretend to be too busy eating my gluten-free oatmeal to answer.

"You're not leaving this table until you tell me." She sits next to me. She's glaring down at me with brown eyes that can see all the way into my soul.

"Okay. If you must know, Crispy and I were playing a game. That's all."

Mom squints at me as if she's deciding whether or not to believe me. "Well, I'm not going to tell you again to stay off Mr. Busselberg's property. It doesn't belong to us anymore."

"I know."

"Don't talk with your mouth full."

After much debate and a few tears, eventually, I persuade Mom that interviewing the neighbors is part of my assignment for the school paper. And even if I'm grounded, I have to do my homework. As a detective or spy or reporter, I need to interview eyewitnesses and find out if they've seen Apollo. The place to start is Mr. Busybody since I know he saw the cub in his herb garden yesterday.

I can't convince Mom to let me skip school to start the interviews right away. She's a stickler for school and morning chores, and I have to promise to clean the petting zoo after my interviews. It's going to be a long day, but I'm determined to find Apollo.

I slop the pig, hand an apple to Raider and a banana to Chewy, then throw some hay over the fence for Spittoon, who thanks me with a sneeze. Maybe Crispy's onto something by taking the camel along to track Apollo. Spittoon is like a radiation detector that goes off near uranium, only he has sneezing fits near cats.

Before my classes start, I pop into the biology lab to check the hair from the shed under the microscope. All the evidence indicates Apollo was there, but it doesn't hurt to confirm with solid proof. Maybe something I found in the shed will tell me how the cub got out—or who let him out.

The yellow hair is definitely not human. Every species has its own distinct scale pattern, almost like a fingerprint. Being the daughter of an animal specialist comes in handy at times like this. The lion's hair looks like a striped ribbon with a thick black center, light border, and dark edges. It has scales like the ones on a yellow snakeskin.

A stray hair catches my attention. It's not like the rest. Instead of a thick band with a black center, it's a thin brown ribbon. It's definitely not human. Maybe it's bat fur. I shudder, remembering my encounter with those nasty flying non-rodents.

The faint musky smell emanating from my pocket reminds me of more evidence I collected last night. I don't need to examine the lilac underpants under the microscope to know that they belong to my doll and that the scat on them belongs to a ferret. I hope the other kids don't think *I* stink. *Aargh.* That's why I've been getting weird looks all morning.

"Hey, Carrot Top, what's that?" Butler catches me holding the incriminating baggie.

"Just examining evidence from the shed where the kidnapper hid Apollo." I drop the baggie into the trash. "And don't call me *Carrot Top.*"

"You found Apollo? He was kidnapped?"

"No and yes."

"What are you doing? Can I help?"

"I don't need your help."

"I didn't say you did." Butler hangs his head like a sad puppy. A firecracker goes off in my brain. "Actually, maybe you can help. You and Oliver."

He gives me a strange look. "Why do you want him?"

"We need a driver."

"Oh, okay," Butler smiles.

After school, Butler and his brother drive me and Crispy to interview the neighbors. On the way, Butler offers us doughnut balls in syrup he calls *gulab jamun*. I almost ask if they're gluten-free but think better of it. What Mom doesn't know won't hurt her. This doughnut ball is so delicious, I regret I didn't get to taste the barfy last time.

Our first stop is Mr. Busybody's. Crispy and the Patel brothers trail me to the front door. When Mrs. Busybody opens the door, I shuffle my feet and have to force myself to make eye contact. I glance behind me at the boys. I didn't expect an audience at my first interview as a reporter.

"Can we ask you a few questions about our cougar cub, Apollo?" I ask, flipping my notebook open.

"You'll want my husband. I didn't see the cougar in the garden, thank goodness." She puts her hand to her chest. "I might have had a heart attack."

"Is Mr. Busy—uh, Busselberg at home?"

"Come on in and have some pie. I'll fetch him from the yard." Mrs. Busybody leads us into the kitchen. After I introduce everyone, she dishes up a plate of cherry pie a la mode for each of us.

We're all sitting around the table, digging in, when Mr. Busybody comes in through the back door. He wipes his brow with a handkerchief and drops into a chair. "So, what can I tell you?" he asks, helping himself to pie.

"Exactly when and where did you see Apollo, our cougar cub?" I take out my notebook again and get ready to write down his answer.

"Well, as you know, I saw him yesterday late afternoon rolling in the catnip plant. Then I called Animal Control. When Agent Killjoy went to look for the lion, he found you trapped in that old shed." Mr. Busselberg wipes his forehead again.

"Did you see what direction Apollo went when he left your garden?" I ask, scribbling notes as fast as I can. I guess it must take practice, because I can't write nearly as fast as he can talk.

"No, but I gave Agent Killjoy the rest of the catnip to use as a lure," he says, his mouth full of pie.

Crispy lets out a gasp, and Freddie does too.

"Agent Killjoy set up a live animal trap out there near the shed in case that big pussycat is still around." Mr. Busybody gestures toward the back door. "He borrowed some stew meat to use as bait."

No! No! No! Alarms go off in my head. We've got to go check that trap ASAP. I snap my notebook shut and push my chair back from the table.

Mom said no more wandering and definitely no more going down to the creek. If I disobey her orders again, I'll probably be grounded until I'm eighteen.

"Thanks, Mr. Busselberg." I stand up and glance around the table. "We'd better be going."

"But I'm not done with my pie." Crispy has a cherry mustache, and so does Freddie.

"Come on." I throw a paper napkin at him. "Let's go find Apollo."

"Cool," Oliver says. "A lion hunt."

"I told you Kassy was fun." Butler smiles at me.

I roll my eyes at Butler, then grab Crispy's arm and pull him up mid-bite.

"Thanks for the delicious pie, Mrs. Busselberg," I say over my shoulder as I drag Crispy out the back door.

23
DROWNED RATS

TRUDGING THROUGH THE WET LEAVES in my sneakers is kind of gross. My socks are soaking wet and my feet are cold. I head back to the shed to find this *live trap*, whatever that is. Crispy and Freddie are on my heels, and the Patel brothers are trailing behind. I hadn't figured on them coming along, but I guess I don't have a choice. They did give us a ride after all.

Just seeing the shed gives me goose bumps. Remembering my night with the bats swarming around my hair gives me the creeps.

"Spread out and look for the trap," I say. "Be careful." I don't exactly know what a live trap is, but it sounds better than a dead one.

Crispy heads toward the forbidden creek while I check behind the shed. Butler runs to catch up to me. His brother just stands there watching us, popping treats into his mouth like he's at the movies.

"Check in those trees," I say to Butler. "I'll look behind the rocks."

"Yes, sir." Butler salutes me and then heads off toward the trees.

If I had a cell phone, I could Google *live trap* to see what we're up against. Apollo's only a cub, but he's a cougar cub. He must weigh nearly twenty pounds by now. So, this trap must be good-sized. Mr. Busybody said they used stew meat. So, I'm assuming they put the meat on a spring inside some kind of cage, and when the cat takes a bite, the door to the cage will slam shut.

I overturn a few rocks with my toe, as if whatever I'm looking for might be under there. The wildflowers are in full bloom, and the forest floor is sprinkled with white blossoms. If Apollo were a horse, he could eat them. But mountain lions are what Mom calls *obligate carnivores*. That means they have to eat meat. Poor Apollo is probably hungry.

I hate to think of Apollo alone out here in the woods. Until yesterday, he was safely hidden in the shed with food and water and bats to eat. I guess the woods are full of potential food if you're a cougar cub. He could eat squirrels and mice and rabbits. And if he's in that horrible trap, at least he's had one good meal of stew meat.

I pick up a long, sturdy stick. I poke the chokecherry bushes to search the undergrowth, and their red berries wave at me. I jump when a grouse flies out of a bush. A squirrel scurries up a tree. But there's no sign of Apollo.

Signs. I should be looking for signs of Apollo and not just for the live trap. After all, Apollo might not be in that trap. He might be on the loose out here, and I need to track him. I scan the ground for tracks and scat. I examine tree trunks for claw marks. A good detective should be able to follow someone's tracks, especially if that someone is a cougar cub.

I bend down to get a closer look at some prints in the mud. Four toes and a pad with two lobes on top and three lobes on the bottom. *Bingo!* It's a lion print!

If it belonged to a dog, it would have toenail prints on the first two toes. Using my stick to brush leaves out of the way, I follow the tracks to a pile of poo. I kneel next to the poo and examine it carefully to see whether or not it's lion scat.

If Apollo has been eating squirrels or rodents, then his scat will contain hair and bones, which make the poo white. I use the baggie as a glove and pick up a piece of whitish poo to take home. Mom will be able to identify it. She's an expert on poop. She's taught me everything I know.

As I'm sliding the sample bag into my spy vest pocket, I hear screaming coming from the creek. I take off running and almost collide with Butler, who is sliding down the creek bank.

Crispy is running alongside the creek, flapping his arms and shouting. The usual furry tail is missing from his neck. "Freddieeeeeee!" he screams, running until he trips over a root and falls flat on his face. *Shih tzu puppy!* That must have hurt.

When I catch up to him, Crispy is sitting beside the creek, blood running down his forehead. I take a wipe from my vest and dab at his face. The creek is at its springtime peak, and the water is moving fast.

He swats my hands away. "Save Freddie! He fell in." Crispy tries to stand up but falls back to the ground.

Butler takes off down the creek. *Holy hurry!* He can run fast.

I wipe more blood off Crispy's face. "Butler will save him," I say, hoping it's true.

"Butler?"

"Look! Freddie's holding on to a branch." I point downstream.

Crispy swivels around in time to see Freddie lose his grip and fall back into the current, and he starts bawling.

What should you do when your eight-year-old brother starts crying his head off? I don't know whether to whack him or hug him. I opt for hugging. It works, and his sobs become sniffles.

Once he calms down, he pushes me away. We both stand up and stare down the creek. Butler is sopping wet, and Freddie is draped over his head, his paws splayed across Butt's forehead. Both are dripping like drowned rats.

Thankfully, Butler is quick on his feet. Sometimes I think Freddie is more trouble than he's worth.

"You saved him!" Crispy claps his hands together, beaming from ear to ear. To him, that stinky ferret is worth the whole world.

24
THE KASSANDRA CURSE

WE'RE A MESSED-UP CREW. My pants are covered in mud from crawling around looking for lion poop. Crispy has crusty blood in his hair and a wicked lump on his forehead. He's not too clean either. Butler and Freddie are both dripping and shivering. Only Oliver is fresh as lettuce. Given the state of our group, I wonder if it's a good idea to keep searching for the live trap. Butler and Freddie will catch colds if they stay out here any longer.

"Butler, why don't you guys take Crispy and Freddie home?" I smile at him for real this time. I have to admit the dude saved Freddie in a pretty heroic rescue. "You'd better go home and dry off too."

"What about you?"

"I'll walk home. It's not that far." I point across the pasture toward our brick house. "I'll take the shortcut."

"Last time you said that, you ended up locked in a shed," Butler says.

Crispy puts his hand to his head. "It hurts. Mom will know what to do. She's a doctor."

"An animal doctor," I say.

"Humans are animals."

He has a point.

"Want some *kaju barfi?*" Oliver holds out a silver container filled with tan triangles that look like Play-Doh.

More barfy. *Why not?* I pick up a wedge and examine it. "What is it?"

"My mom makes it from cashews and sugar," Butler says. "The grand opening of her bakery is next Monday."

"Gluten-free?"

He nods.

Except for the sugar, even Mom would approve of barfy. I take a tiny bite off the corner. "Hey, it's pretty good."

"Told you." Butler smiles.

Crispy's already sharing his second barfy with Freddie, who's wrapped around his neck and dripping all over his jacket.

"I hate to just leave you here." Butler looks pathetic with a lock of wet hair dribbling down his face.

"I'll be fine. Go dry off before you catch a cold."

"Text me when you get home?" Butler asks with those sad puppy eyes.

Sigh. What's wrong with this guy? "Go!" I don't tell him Mom won't let me have a cell phone, so I can't text or call, Google or Instagram, or anything else like a normal kid.

Once the boys are gone, I continue my search for the live trap and Apollo. I beat more bushes, kick more leaves, examine more tree trunks. Nothing.

Disappointed, I climb the fence and start across the pasture toward our house. An expanse of green spreads in every direction: the grass, the trees, the bushes. Everything in Tennessee is green.

About halfway across the pasture, a blinding flash hits my eyes. I pick up my pace. Something shiny reflects the sunlight. As I get closer, I make out a rectangular metal cage. I race up to it and stop short. Its weird-looking, *V*-shaped double door is open like the jaws of a metallic shark. I bend down to take a closer look. The raw meat inside is covered with ants. *Disgusting.*

Too bad I don't have my telescopic pointer anymore. I dropped my sturdy stick long ago. And there are no sticks to be found in the pasture. I've got to get the meat out and spring the trap. I try to lift the cage, but it's too heavy. It's big enough that I could fit inside. It must be for a Saint Bernard or a Great Dane, something bigger than a cougar cub.

I sit down on top of it, wondering what to do next. Since I can't move it, do I dare crawl inside to get the bait? I can't just leave it here waiting for poor hungry Apollo to find, looking for a free meal. I wonder if the ants are enough to discourage him. Probably not. He might even like eating ants. To a cougar cub, ants might be like frosting on a cake.

Maybe I can crawl in just far enough to grab the meat and go. It's risky because I'm not sure what springs the trap. I walk around the cage again to see if I can figure it out. There must be a trigger mechanism under the bait, so when the animal eats it, the door shuts. If I could lift the cage, I could just tip the meat out. I try again. No way. I continue making circles around it. No wonder I can't move it—the cage is staked into the ground. This thing isn't going anywhere.

Maybe if I crawl in just far enough to inspect the weird door, I can figure out how it works. I drop to my hands and knees at the entrance to the cage. There are two doors hooked together to form the V. They're open with barely enough room for me to scoot inside the cage. There's a large silver plate on the bottom of the cage and then the ant-covered meat at the back. I'm guessing eating the meat is what triggers the trap. So as long as I don't touch the meat, I should be okay.

I move a tiny bit forward. Now my head is inside. The steel bars of the cage are pressing into my hands. I slide one knee inside and then the other. I take a breath and hold it. Nothing happens, thank goodness. Okay, I just have to figure out how this door works without touching the meat. I scoot forward another couple of inches.

Bam! When my hand leans on the metal plate, the door slams shut. *Turnip greens!* I'm locked in. *Not again!* I can't believe it. That was so stupid. If I could move, I'd whack myself in the head for being such an idiot. *Aaaaahhhh!* I feel like screaming. I'm such a dummy. I'm trapped in an animal cage. Okay, I'm officially freaking out again.

Breathe in, breathe out. Breathe in, breathe out. That's what Mom says when I'm hyperventilating. *Slow your breath down. In and out. In and out.* It's not working. I can hardly move. The metal cage is digging into my hands and knees. My heart is pounding like there's a gorilla in my chest.

Calm down. Concentrate. Use your human-sized brain. You are not just any animal. There must be a way for a human to open this. I can figure this out. I just have to breathe and focus. But it's not so easy to breathe and focus when you're trapped in a cage the size of a small coffin.

I think of my English teacher, Mr. Whittaker, telling me the mythological Kassandra, my namesake, died in a cage. I asked you before if you believe in fate. I escaped fate once. Can I do it again? Or is it my destiny to die locked in this animal trap?

25
SUPPER WITH APOLLO

FROM THE INSIDE, THIS CAGE DOESN'T SEEM as big as it did from the outside. It's kind of claustrophobic in here. If I had a cell phone, I could Google *how to open a live trap.* But I'd better not use that particular argument on Mom. I've learned it's best to keep Mom on a need-to-know basis. And she definitely doesn't need to know I'm locked in a cage. Unfortunately, she always manages to find out things like this anyway. It's like she has a sixth sense for this kind of stuff, the kind of stuff I'm not supposed to be doing. I glance down at my sleeve. If Mom's sixth sense doesn't give me away, the giant hole in my brand-new cotton shirt will.

159

I can barely turn around, let alone stand up, and it's totally freaking me out. My heart is racing. I take a deep breath. "Calm down. Calm down," I tell myself.

At least the sun is still shining, and I have another hour before it gets dark. If I weren't stuck in this cage, it would be a beautiful spring day. My mind is spinning, mostly with regret. Why didn't I notice Crispy's obsession with my newspaper story before it was too late? Why couldn't I find Apollo and save the zoo? Why am I always doing stupid stuff like getting trapped in sheds and locked in cages? *Earth to Kassy.* Maybe Dad is right.

Mrs. Cheever says reporters don't doubt themselves, because they're confident and clever, and that's how they get the job done. It's not too late for me to be a doer. I just need to use my brain to figure out what to do and how to do it.

Dad says I overthink things and I should jump in instead of sitting on the sidelines thinking all the time. But if I don't think about what I'm doing, then how will I know it's the right thing to do? If I jump without thinking, how will I know where I'll land? I exhale out loud. *Earth to Kassy.*

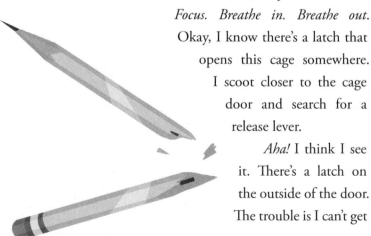

Focus. Breathe in. Breathe out. Okay, I know there's a latch that opens this cage somewhere. I scoot closer to the cage door and search for a release lever.

Aha! I think I see it. There's a latch on the outside of the door. The trouble is I can't get my hand through the metal bars to reach it. Maybe I have something in my vest I can use. I pat my pockets, wishing my retractable pointer wasn't still stuck on the roof of the shed. Maybe I can reach it with my pencil? I pry the pencil between the spokes of the cage. I can't get enough leverage to move the latch. I push as hard as I can. *Shrimp and grits!* My pencil snaps in half.

Out of breath, I lean against the side of the cage and stare out at the pasture, wondering what to do next. On the bright side, it's daylight and there are no bats in sight. The day is warm, but the metal bars of the cage are cool and sharp against my back and bottom.

Wait! Are those furry ears poking up out of the grass? I sit up and hit my head against the top of the cage. *Ouch! Yes!* It's him. It's Apollo!

"Apollo, here, boy." I pick up a slimy piece of stew meat, shake off the ants, and poke it out through the bars of the cage. "Dinner. Apolloooo." Holding the meat between my thumb and finger, I wave it in the air.

The grass sways as the ears get closer. Apollo's little lion face appears out of the weeds and stares at me with a bewildered look.

"Apollo!" I'm so happy to see him I could hug him, if only I weren't in this stupid cage. "You're okay. You're here." My whole body smiles at the sight of him, with those adorable tufts of fur coming out of his ears and those long black whiskers. "Apollo, you silly cub."

I wave the meat again, but he's skeptical. Unlike me, he knows better than to come near a cage. "Good boy." I drop the piece of meat outside the cage and pick up another piece. I

dangle it out through the bars. Apollo saunters over and grabs it with a claw. He throws it in the air a couple of times and then scarfs it down, purring.

"Apollo. Where have you been?" If only he could spring me from this cage. He needs opposable thumbs. I bet Chewy the chimp could do it. *Aargh.* I'm thinking like Crispy again. Anyway, I have opposable thumbs, and a lot of good it's doing me.

I push the rest of the meat out through the bars. At least I can give Apollo a nice supper. He gobbles it down and sits next to the cage, washing his face with his paw. He must like ants, because he ate them too.

I laugh with relief. Agent Stinkerton Killjoy didn't capture our cub. He's safe here with me. Someone will come looking for me, and they'll find us here together. I just hope it's soon.

"Apollo, you little rascal. You gave us all quite a scare." I stick my finger out of the cage and wiggle it at the cub. He glances over and then goes back to his bath.

Suddenly, Apollo's head whips from side to side. I follow his gaze upward and see a butterfly. He takes off after it.

"Apollo, come back!" I yell. "No!"

I watch him disappear into the grass at the far edge of the pasture.

"Noooooo! Come back. Please."

Nooooo! The evil Stinkerton Killjoy appears out of the trees and throws a big canvas bag at the ground. Something is wriggling under the canvas. *Oh no! No, no, no!* He's bagged Apollo.

"Nooooo!" I shout. I watch helplessly as Killjoy wrestles with the bag, throws it over his shoulder, and disappears back into the trees.

I slump back against the cold steel cage. The bright side just got a whole lot dimmer. It's hopeless. Agent Killjoy has Apollo. And he's already got an injunction to close down the petting zoo. I've really messed up this time. How can I face Mom and Crispy if we lose the zoo? What will we do? I pinch my arm really hard to keep myself from crying. A pink welt blooms on my skin. I kick at the cage, but that only makes the metal bars poke into my butt even more.

"Help!" I shout into the empty pasture.

For something to take my mind off my misery, I close my eyes and imagine myself back at home, lying on my bed, reading a Nancy Drew mystery with a plate of fresh chocolate cookies and a cold glass of milk on my nightstand. Yeah, cookies and milk are a fantasy at my house. Gluten-free dog biscuits and milk made from nuts is my reality.

When I open my eyes, Butler is standing over the cage, gaping down at me.

"Don't sneak up on me!" I sit up and hit my head against the top of the cage. "I almost had a heart attack."

"What are you doing in there?"

"Just get me out," I say, rolling my eyes.

Butler presses a lever, and the cage door opens. "The second O'Roarke I've rescued today."

I have to admit, I'm happy to see him. I crawl out on my hands and knees. Wobbly from being folded into a pretzel for so long, I take Butler's hand and let him help me up. "How'd you know I was here?"

"When you didn't text, I came looking for you."

"Where's Oliver?"

"He's waiting in the car."

"I hope he brought more barfy."

Butler is laughing. His laughter is catching, and I start laughing too.

Then I remember Agent Killjoy and Apollo and I want to cry. "Animal Control got Apollo." Saying it out loud makes it seem more real. A tear rolls down my cheek, and I wipe it off with the torn sleeve of my shirt.

"You don't know that. We'll find—"

"I do! I saw Agent Killjoy catch him and put him in a bag." I'm fighting back sobs.

"What?"

"Apollo smelled the stew meat and came over to the cage." I can barely get the words out. I've got to pull myself together. I don't want Butler to see me cry. "After I gave him the meat, he ran after a butterfly, and then Killjoy came out of the trees and bagged him." I got into this, and I'm going to get out. I stretch my arms and legs. It's not too late. I've got to get Apollo back and save the zoo. I'm determined. "Let's see if we can catch up to him before he gets back to the dog pound."

"Can't your mom just go to the pound and get Apollo back?"

"Killjoy says he filed an injunction." When I say it out loud, my eyes burn like I'm going to cry again. I dig my fingernails into my arm and squeeze my eyes tightly. "He wants to take Apollo away from us and shut down the petting zoo."

"He can't do that!"

"I hope not." I take off running toward my house.

"This way!" Butler shouts after me. "The car is in front of Mr. Busselberg's."

I ignore him and just keep running as fast as I can. Within a few seconds, he catches up to me. I keep going, my legs pumping faster and faster. Butler is running alongside me.

"Oliver can take us to Animal Control if you want," Butler says. "Or we can go look for the dogcatcher's van."

I stop in my tracks. That's not a bad idea. Maybe we can catch up to Killjoy before he gets back to Animal Control.

Oliver drives us around, looking for the yellow Animal Control van, for an hour. By the time Oliver drops me off at home after our futile chase, it's dark and raining. He says goodbye and hands me a box with a picture of a big black phone and some writing on it. "Something so you can call me if you need help."

"Mom won't let me have a phone." I hand the box back to Butler.

"It's not a phone. It's a walkie-talkie."

"I don't know—" I try to give it back, but he shakes his head and folds his arms over his chest.

Carrying the box under my arm, I sneak in through the side door and tiptoe up the stairs. If Mom catches me, I'll be grounded for life.

"Kassandra Urania O'Roarke!"

I'm halfway up the stairs. I stop in my tracks.

Chicken-fried steak! Busted again.

HONING OUR SKILLS

WHAT HAPPENS NEXT IS WAY WORSE than being grounded for
life. Mom makes me sit next to her while she talks to Dad on
speakerphone. I stare at a crack on the floor, wishing I could
crawl into it.

Mom tells Dad about the shed and the cage, and Dad tells
her about catching me stealing Ronny's coloring book.

"Well?" Mom asks. "What do you have to say for yourself?"

I want to explain and apologize, but no words come out.
My voice is frozen. It's like the connection between my brain
and my mouth is blocked off. I can hear the words *I'm sorry* in
my head, but they won't come out of my mouth. *I'm sorry. I'm
sorry for being born.* My face is burning, and tears are streaming

down my cheeks. It's like I've forgotten how to talk. No sound comes out of my mouth.

After she gets off the phone with Dad, Mom makes me sit there while she calls my school. She makes an appointment for me to see the counselor. She says it will be good for me, but it feels like punishment. Now I'm going to have to explain my existence to yet another adult. Even if I could make the words come out, no one would believe me. Anyway, how's a counselor going to help get Apollo back, and Dad back, and my life back?

Mom decides to send us to Dad's a day early for our weekend visit. I think she can't deal with us anymore. I'm not looking forward to another long weekend with Rotten Ronny giving me the stink eye like I'm some sort of thief.

Facing Dad right now is just too much. My eyes sting, and my stomach is swirling. Mom says I need "a more structured environment," whatever that means. You'd think it might mean she'd drive us downtown, but no. She still makes us take the city bus. Sometimes parents are hard to figure out.

It doesn't help that I'm still not speaking to my brother. I won't even sit with him on the bus. We ride in silence, him in the very front and me in the very back. For the whole ten-minute ride, I try not to think about how much Mom and Dad hate me. Instead, I concentrate on how I'm going to get Apollo back and save the petting zoo. Forget about my stupid newspaper story. If I can rescue our cub, then maybe Mom and Dad will forgive me.

Mom tried to get Apollo back from Animal Control, but Killjoy wouldn't budge. He says the petting zoo is a safety hazard, and it doesn't matter that Mom saved the baby cougar's life when a hunter brought it to the clinic after killing its mother. Mom says she won't give up until she gets Apollo back, even if she has to sue the city and Stinky personally.

When we get to Dad's town house, Zeus and Mari greet us with more cookies and candy. Her sideways glance at me is the only giveaway she's still upset about the coloring book incident. I'm half tempted to tell her Crispy's the one who's been taking stuff, not me . . . well, except the coloring book. It would serve him right after everything he's done. But I'm not a snitch.

Mari smiles and holds out the plate of cookies. As usual, Crispy digs in with both hands. And as usual, Ronny is in her game room watching TV and munching on cookies.

"Whatcha watching?" Crispy asks.

"*Chicken Run.*" Ronny points to the plate of cookies.

I shake my head, but Crispy grabs two and then plops down in an easy chair. He breaks a piece off a cookie and offers it to Freddie, who, as usual, is curled around his neck.

"Since you don't eat chickens, you'll like this movie," Ronny says. "The chickens are trying to escape." She points at the screen. "That rooster, Rocky, is going to help them break out of prison."

"That's a farm, not a prison," I say. I take my detective novel out of my backpack and try to tune out the stupid cartoon.

"Not if you're a chicken." Crispy takes another cookie and puts it in his pocket, which is already stuffed with Kit Kats.

I glance at the TV. Crispy has a point. It looks like the chickens *are* in jail. Makes me think of Animal Control and the concrete cell Apollo is locked in right now. Poor little guy.

"Don't worry. They break out," Ronny says. "I've seen it before."

Break out. "That's it!" I grab a cookie and take a bite. "We need to break Apollo out of Animal Control!" I wave the cookie in the air in triumph and then finish it in two bites. *Holy hazelnut!* The cookie is almost as good as Mrs. Patel's barfy. I take another one to help me concentrate on a plan to spring our cub.

"Can I come?" Ronny asks.

"No!"

"But I've got special skills that might help."

"Like what?"

"See that palm leaf?" She points to a giant plant in the corner.

"Yeah."

"Watch this." Ronny stands up and dropkicks her soccer ball, and the palm leaf goes flying. The ball hits the wall and bounces back to her. Her mother's not going to be happy about Ronny wrecking the plant, but she's a pretty good shot.

"Wow," Crispy says. "I bet you can't hit that star." He points to a flag on the wall.

"I'm not kicking the star in the Cuban flag." She dropkicks the ball. "How about the apple on that poster?" The ball smacks into the apple and bounces back to her like a boomerang.

"What are you kids doing?" Mari pokes her head into the room.

"Sorry, Mari," I say with a smirk. "My fault."

"Figures," she says under her breath. She must think I'm hard of hearing. "Keep it down, okay? Your dad's on the phone."

She glares at Ronny. "And no kicking that ball in the house." She disappears from the doorway.

I hate to admit it, but Ronny is a crack shot with a soccer ball. You never know when a well-aimed soccer ball might come in handy on a dangerous mission like breaking a cougar cub out of the dog pound. "Okay, you're in."

"What about me?" Crispy asks.

"What's your special skill?" I ask. I'm still mad at Crispy for causing this mess in the first place.

Crispy shrugs. "I guess I don't have any special skills."

"You're good at eating cookies," Ronny offers.

"And how will eating cookies help us on our mission to save Apollo?" I ask.

"If there's a giant wall of cookies blocking our path, Crispy can eat his way through it."

"Ha!" I scoff. "Cookie-eating doesn't count." She's as nutty as he is. Cookie walls, talking animals, what's next?

Red blotches bloom on Crispy's face, a sure sign he's getting ready to cry. I must be a softy, because I feel sorry for the little orangutan, even though it's because of him I almost died in a bat-infested shed, ended up locked in a cage, and alienated my whole family. "You talk to animals. That's your special skill."

He eyes me suspiciously.

"The ability to communicate with animals could really come in handy on a mission to Animal Control."

Crispy's face lights up.

"If we run into a wall of dogs, you can ask them to move." I wink at him.

"What about Freddie?" he asks. "What's his special skill?"

I laugh thinking about Freddie's special skill.

Mari appears again. "What are you kids doing now?"

We're all giggling.

"What's going on?" Mari asks.

Crispy laughs so hard he spits out his cookie.

"Are you okay?" Mari pats him on the back. Freddie swings around and gives her the business end.

"That ferret is sick," Mari says, blinking and covering her nose.

Freddie must know she's talking about him. He jumps down and helps himself to another cookie.

"Freddie, that's not polite," Crispy says, picking him up. Freddie ferrets out of Crispy's grasp and runs off toward the kitchen. He comes back carrying a set of keys in his mouth.

Mari chases him around the room. They're whirling around each other like a Tennessee tornado.

Freddie finally jumps back up onto Crispy's shoulders and then drops the keys into my brother's hand.

"Stealing keys!" I grab the keys and give them back to Mari. "That's Freddie's special skill."

27

ASSEMBLING THE TEAM

IT TAKES A WHILE TO CONVINCE Mari and Dad to let Ronny come home with us after breakfast. But tomorrow is Memorial Day, and it's a school holiday.

I tell Dad and Mari we're working together on my newspaper story, which is sort of true. I mean, rescuing Apollo will make a great story. Assuming we succeed.

When I call Mom to ask if it's okay to bring Ronny home with us for an overnight, she's confused, like she doesn't know who I'm taking about. I hate to rub salt in the Dad-sized hole in her heart, so I say Ronny is a friend of Crispy's from soccer. Well, that's true too, right?

Mari makes Dad drive us home because she doesn't want Ronny to take the bus, not even for ten minutes. I told you she's spoiled. I'm glad because we get home in half the time, and we need every minute we can get to plan the jailbreak and practice our special skills.

I lead my team up to my bedroom and lock the door. The three of us—well, four if you count Freddie—sit in a circle on my floor.

Distracted by my piles of books and stacks of spy stuff around my room, Ronny won't sit still. "You're such a slob," she says, riffling through my *Spy* magazines.

Whatever. I roll my eyes. "Concentrate on the task at hand."

She spins her soccer ball on one finger. "A soccer ball kicked to the head can knock someone out," she says with a mischievous grin. Seems Ronny has a violent streak—maybe that's why she broke her blue crayon on Dora's face.

"Hopefully we won't need to knock someone out," I say. Although if we do, I'll be glad to have her along. I imagine her kicking a soccer ball into Agent Stinkerton Killjoy's fat head. It would serve him right for kidnapping Apollo.

I fetch a sketch pad from my desk, along with a couple of colored pencils, and then sit cross-legged on the carpet. Leaning against my canopy bed, I draw the layout of Animal Control from memory.

Crispy and Ronny are rolling the soccer ball back and forth on the floor.

"Here's the building." I hold up my drawing.

"Looks like SpongeBob SquarePants," Ronny says, giggling.

"So I'm not an artist." I think of her Dora coloring book. She's a fine one to talk. She can't even color in the lines. By the looks of the page I found in the petting zoo, she doesn't even try. "Everyone has their strengths and weaknesses," I say.

"And their special skills," Crispy joins in.

"Right. And we need to put our special skills together to break Apollo out of prison." I put the sketch pad on the floor in the middle of our circle and use my pencil as a pointer, since my retractable pointer is still stuck in the roof of that disgusting bat shed.

"Let's build an airplane and fly him out," Crispy says.

"Let's not and say we did."

"That's what they did in *Chicken Run*," Ronny says.

"We're not chickens. And we're not building a plane."

"Chickens can't fly, and neither can we," Crispy says. "That's why we need a plane."

"Rocks can't fly either, but that doesn't make us rocks." Under my breath, I add, "Except maybe you."

"Books can't fly, and we're not books," Ronny says.

"Okay, we're not chickens, rocks, or books. Now, can we get back to our plan?" I point to a rectangle on my sketch. "This is the reception desk where Angelica Dworfman stands guard. She likes chocolate. A fact we will use to our advantage."

"Everyone likes chocolate," Ronny says.

"Yeah, but she drinks hers in Starbucks coffee with whipped cream on top."

"How do you know?" Crispy asks.

"Didn't you notice her whipped cream mustache and the mocha smell on her breath when we went to get Freddie last week?"

Crispy shakes his head.

"That's not all. She likes her mocha with a flaky croissant."

"A what?" Ronny asks.

"It's a pastry like a fluffy dinner roll. She had flakes all down her sweater."

Crispy and Ronny look at me like I'm speaking Klingon. Although I'm sure Crispy watches enough *Star Trek* to be fluent in Klingon.

"We're going to bribe her with treats."

They exchange confused glances.

I point to my drawing again. "The cages are back here." I tap my pencil on a series of squares in the corner of the sketch pad. "We have to get into the back of the building and then rescue Apollo without anyone catching us."

"We could dress up like Agent Killjoy." Crispy puffs out his cheeks.

I shake my head. Working with these two is going to be tough.

"We need a driver." I open my desk drawer and pull out the present Butler gave me. Inside the box, I find a walkie-talkie, a charging dock, and a set of instructions. "*Shih tzu puppy!* It has to charge for at least an hour." I glance at my spy watch. Noon. "I wonder when Animal Control closes."

"What is it?" Ronny asks, picking up the walkie-talkie and turning it over.

I grab it out of her hands and plug it into its dock. "A walkie-talkie. Butler gave it to me so I could call him."

"Why don't you just call him on the phone?" Crispy asks.

Hey, why didn't I think of that? Sometimes the simplest solutions are the hardest to see. I hold my hand up for a high five. Then I realize I don't know his phone number. "Go see where Mom is while I look for an old phone book."

Holy hundreds! There are pages of Patels. It's hopeless. Who knew there were so many Patels in Lemontree Heights? We'll have to wait for the walkie-talkie to charge.

In the meantime, I restock my spy vest with the essentials for a jailbreak: a big handful of pennies, some dog biscuits, and a baggie stuffed full of raw hamburger. I press hard on my pocket's Velcro seal. I'm not used to carrying raw meat in my spy vest, and I don't want it to fall out. Of course, I also have the usual: baggies, tape, scissors, string, and emergency granola bars.

Next, I read the instructions on the walkie-talkie. I set it up and wait. I pace around my room. It's not as easy as it sounds since my bedroom has piles of stuff everywhere. Crispy and Ronny went outside to play with the soccer ball—our secret weapon.

The minute the hour is up, I lift the walkie-talkie from its base, turn it on, dial up the volume, and press the button. "Hello, Butler?"

I release the button and wait for his response. According to the instructions, unlike phones, walkie-talkies allow only one person to talk at a time.

No response. I push the button again. "Butler, are you there?"

When I release it, I hear static and then Butler's voice. "What's up, Carrot?"

"We're going to fetch Apollo, and we need your brother to drive. And don't call me *Carrot*." I glance at my spy watch. It's just after one o'clock. "I checked and Animal Control closes at four on Sundays," I say into the mouthpiece.

"Kassy, are you still there?"

I realize I forgot to push the button down. I press it and try again. "Can you ask your brother and come over ASAP?"

"He's at my mom's bakery getting ready for the grand opening tomorrow."

Biscuits and gravy! Now what? How will we rescue Apollo?

Wait. That's the perfect cover story. I'll tell Mom we're going to help Mrs. Patel set up her new bakery. Even if I'm grounded, this plan will appeal to Mom's desire to help people . . . and all other creatures.

"Where's the bakery?"

"It's on Main Street. You can't miss it. Patel's Pastries." Butler's voice is scratchy and sounds weird from the walkie-talkie static.

"Meet me at the bakery." I glance at my watch again. "Hurry, we're running out of time."

28
THE PLAN

I LOOK AT MY WATCH. It's almost two. The clock is ticking. And I still need to gather the team and rehearse the plan.

Mom drops us off at Patel's Pastries. She's so busy she forgot we're supposed to be grounded. I knew she would. After a couple days of steaming, she always cools off.

Patel's Pastries is in the center of the Lemontree Heights business district. It's a super cute little shop with a pink-and-yellow awning. I peek inside the window and see tile-topped tables, a stack of colorful chairs, and a pastry case in back... but I don't see Butler.

I push the button and talk into the walkie-talkie. "Butler, where are you? We're at the bakery. Do you copy?"

I hear scratchy static and then Butler's voice. "Copy that. On my way. Riding my bike. Almost there." He sounds out of breath.

I push the button down again to tell him to hurry. I glance up Main Street and see him pedaling, his legs whizzing around like a propeller. He's going faster than the cars.

When he skids to a stop in front of the bakery, his cheeks have a pink glow. "So, what's the plan?" he asks, panting.

"Can you guys drive us to Animal Control?" I ask.

"You can drive?" Ronny asks. "I'm Veronica, by the way."

"My brother, Oliver, has his license." He rolls his eyes. "He thinks he's so cool."

"We don't have time for this." I tug on Butler's sleeve and pull him toward the entrance to the bakery. "See if your brother will drive us."

"Sorry, he's out getting supplies for the grand opening." Butler holds the door open. "I'll ask Mom if she can take us."

Single file, we follow Butler into the bakery and then into the back where his Mom is cooking. *Holy honey bun!* The kitchen smells sticky and delicious. My mouth waters thinking about Mrs. Patel's desserts. So far, barfy is my favorite.

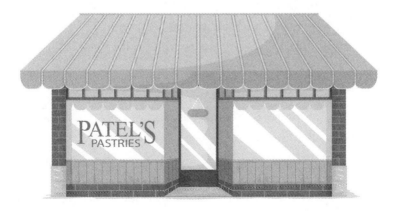

"Mom, can you take us to pick up Apollo?" Butler asks.

"Peanut, not now, I have a *baath* in the oven." Mrs. Patel is dashing around the kitchen with an oven mitt on her hand. She grabs a jar off a shelf and shakes a couple of weird-looking pods into her chubby hand.

"You take a bath in the oven?" Ronny asks.

"Peanut?" I poke Butler in the shoulder. *Ha-ha.* He has an embarrassing nickname, too.

"*Baath* is coconut cake," Butler says, ignoring me.

"I love coconut!" Ronny's eyes widen.

"Mrs. Patel," I say in my sweetest voice. "Can you drive us?"

"Sweetie, I can't leave a cake in the oven or it will burn up." Mrs. Patel zips around the kitchen, patting dough, stirring pots, sprinkling powdered sugar. It's like watching a magic show. "Tell you what. You kids help me set up the café tables and chairs in the front, and when Oliver gets back, he can drive you to pick up your friend."

"When will Oliver be back?" I ask.

Mrs. Patel checks her timer. "Thirty-eight minutes until the cake is done." When she wipes her forehead with the back of her hand, she leaves a trail of dusty flour across her brown skin. "Oliver should be back by then."

Thirty-eight minutes! I set my spy watch timer. The dog pound will be nearly closed by then. I hope we make it in time.

"You kids want some *chai*?" Mrs. Patel's round cheeks are flushed, and strands of black hair have escaped from the bun at the back of her neck.

"Shy?" Ronny asks. She knows nothing about being shy, that's for sure.

182

"Spiced tea with sugar and milk." Mrs. Patel hands out small paper cups of thick, milky tea poured from a big metal coffeepot.

The tea is warm and sweet and reassuring. After we gulp our tea, we head back to the storefront. We unstack chairs and set them around café tables.

I check my watch. Twenty-five more minutes. Ever notice how time seems to slow down when you're waiting for something? *This is going to be the longest twenty-five minutes of my life.*

Mrs. Patel hands one towel to me and another to Butler. "Would you mind wiping off the glass pastry case?" She brings out a broom and gives it to Crispy. "And maybe you could sweep?" She turns to Ronny. "Veronica, can you help me stir the stuffing for the *puran poli?*" Mrs. Patel has taken a liking to Ronny.

"What's *puran poli?*" Ronny asks as she follows Mrs. Patel back into the kitchen.

"Sweet stuffed flatbread. I'll fry it fresh . . ." Her voice trails off as she disappears into the back.

Oliver bursts through the front door, his arms full of paper bags. Butler and I jump out of his way as he barrels through toward the back.

"Coming through," Oliver says as he whizzes past and heads into the kitchen.

When he's out of earshot, Butler asks, "What's the plan?"

"You bribe the receptionist with Starbucks while Crispy uses my spare change to distract the girl who cleans out the cages. Freddie snags the keys to the back door, and then I grab Apollo." I wipe the glass case again for good measure. "Easy peasy." Of course, it *won't* be easy, especially if Agent Stinkerton

Killjoy is anywhere on the premises. That's where Ronny's soccer skills could come in handy. "But we have to get there before they close."

Ding! I rush into the kitchen in time to see Oliver helping Mrs. Patel remove a giant sheet cake from the oven. Both of them are wearing big blue-and-yellow-striped oven mitts.

"I'll just help Mom put this on a rack to cool and then we can go." Oliver helps Mrs. Patel slide the cake onto a wire rack.

"When you get back, you can try it," Mrs. Patel says with a smile.

"Can we stop at Starbucks?" I ask Oliver.

He shrugs.

"What could you possibly want there when you've got chai and cake here?" Mrs. Patel asks, blowing a stray hair out of her face.

"True! Mrs. P., can we take some tea and cake to our friend?" I ask.

Mrs. Patel's tea and dessert would cast a spell on even the most serious Starbucks addict.

"The cake is still hot." Mrs. Patel grabs a knife, cuts a square in the corner of the pan, and then uses a spatula to lift the golden cake into an aluminum to-go box. "Peanut, get a couple of to-go cups for the chai." She points to the counter next to the giant tea urn.

"Can I try the cake?" Ronny asks, clapping her hands.

"When we get back, we can celebrate." I say as I take a cup of chai from Butler. "Let's go. We don't have much time." I glance at my watch. *Chai and barfy!* It's after three o'clock. "Come on, guys. Get a move on!"

29
JAIL BREAK

IN THE CAR ON THE WAY TO ANIMAL CONTROL, I go over the plan. Everyone has a part to play. And timing is crucial. I'm worried about Crispy and Ronny. They're having too much fun and not concentrating.

Butler's brother seems okay, but I'm whispering just in case. He doesn't need to know he's driving the getaway car for a jailbreak. I repeat my instructions again for my goofy brother and Rotten Ronny, who are sitting next to me in the back-seat wrestling over the soccer ball.

I'm surprised when Oliver turns around and asks, "What's my part?"

I just stare at him. Then I have an idea. "You can tell the receptionist about your mom's new bakery and give her the chai and cake as samples." Since he's older, this is even better than my original plan of having Ronny try to pull it off. "Just keep her busy while we sneak around to the back and rescue Apollo." If Angelica Dworfman likes sweets, she'll love Mrs. Patel's pastries.

He smiles and nods. "I can advertise Mom's bakery." For a teenager, Oliver is pretty cool.

Oliver pulls into the parking lot in front of Animal Control. "Now what?" he asks.

"Actually, you'd better stay with the getaway car in case we need to make a quick break for it," I say, reconsidering the plan.

"Cool." He nods. "I'll drive the getaway car."

"Butler, you take the treats in to distract Angelica Dworfman."

"Roger that," Butler says. He opens the passenger door and slides out of the front seat, balancing the tea on top of the cake box. He shuts the door with his foot and heads toward the entrance.

"Drive around back," I say to Oliver.

So, here's the plan: Ronny, Crispy, and Freddie will go in the front door a few minutes after Butler goes in with the treats. Crispy is wearing a baseball hat and sunglasses, posing as a boy wanting to adopt a dog. That's not hard for him since he wants to adopt every animal he sees. When the attendant takes Crispy back to meet the dogs, he'll "accidentally" drop the baggie full of pennies. Counting on normal human reaction, the attendant will help him pick them all up. While she's doing that, Ronny will sneak off to open the back door for me, and then I'll find Apollo and make a break for it.

If all goes according to plan, Butler will be chatting with the receptionist while she scarfs down Mrs. Patel's treats, and

Crispy will keep the attendant busy with the penny ploy while Apollo and I walk right out the back door. Easy peasy.

If Agent Killjoy shows up, Ronny will have to use her soccer ball to knock him out so we can escape. *What could go wrong?*

Once we're parked near the back door, I scan the parking lot. I don't see any signs of Killjoy or his van, so I hop out of the car, and the others follow to the back door.

"Ronny, use your soccer ball to take out the security camera." I point to the electronic eye staring at us.

Ronny dropkicks the ball, and it slams into the camera, cracking the glass eye. So far, so good.

"You guys remember what you're supposed to do?"

Ronny and Crispy nod. Freddie does too.

"Go around front. Get in quickly. Drop the pennies. And then open the back door."

Everything is ticking along like clockwork. Oliver stays with the getaway car, motor running. Ronny, Crispy, and Freddie zip around the corner of the building.

Now I wait. If my stomach had legs it would be doing backflips. I put my ear to the door and listen for the pennies to drop. *Holy hoarfrost!* That metal door is cold.

My walkie-talkie squelches to life. Startled, I jump back.

"We're in," Ronny says.

I press the button. "Roger that," I respond.

Even through the heavy door, I hear the pennies skittle across the concrete floor. I hold my breath. Hopefully, they distract the attendant long enough for Ronny to get to the back door without anyone noticing. Hopefully, Angelica Dworfman is still enjoying Mrs. Patel's chai and cake. My stomach grumbles.

Oliver rolls down the SUV window and yells, "What's taking so long?"

I turn and put my fingers to my lips. "Shhhh."

The door swings open and bangs right into my head. *Shrimp and grits!* That hurt. Holding my head, I scoot inside the dog pound. Row after row of cages hold canine captives inside. *Holy harmony!* Dozens of dogs bark a discordant symphony that can probably be heard all the way to Nashville.

I slide up the first aisle, scanning the cages for our cougar cub. No cub. *Shhh!* The dogs are making quite a ruckus. I expected natural human reaction, but not quite so much natural canine reaction. I toss out dog biscuits as I go. Not even Mrs. Patel's cake will be enough to keep Angelica Dworfman or the attendant from investigating this racket. *Red beans and rice!* I should have brought more dog biscuits.

Rounding the corner into the next aisle, I smack right into the attendant. I glance at her name tag. People are always nicer if you use their names. "Sorry about that, Briana." I hold up a dog biscuit.

"How'd you get in here?" Briana's springy curls are bouncing up and down from our collision. A purple bruise is blossoming under her right eye. My hard head must have rammed right into her cheekbone.

Brussels sprouts! My plan is falling apart. I improvise a backup plan and try the direct approach. Maybe her pain will act as a truth serum. "Where's the cougar cub?"

"What?"

"I heard you captured a lion, and I came to see him."

"This isn't a zoo."

"True. More like a prison."

"What?" Briana asks. "Did you check in at the front desk?" She's still holding her head. I hope I didn't give her a concussion.

As if on cue, Angelica Dworfman appears, cake crumbs down the front of her sweater. "What's going on?" She does a double take. "Oh, it's you. The one with the ferret."

A musky smell announces the arrival of Crispy and Freddie. "Speak of the deviled egg," I say.

Ronny and her soccer ball join us. Now at least we've got the advantage.

"She's asking about the cougar cub," the attendant says, rubbing her bruised cheek.

"Agent Killjoy left with him not fifteen minutes ago," says Angela Dworfman. "We're about to close. You kids need to leave."

Killjoy left with Apollo. *No!* My stomach feels like I swallowed a bag of rocks.

Crispy looks at me with fear in his eyes. "Where'd he take Apollo?"

"I don't know what you're up to, but I'm sure it's no good." The receptionist points at Crispy. "Where are your parents?"

"Actually, he's an orphan," I say. "He lost his parents in a house fire."

"Tragic, I'm sure—" The receptionist is interrupted by the arrival of Butler.

"Did you get him?" Butler asks, a half-eaten piece of sheet cake in his hand. "Can we go?"

"Not until we find Apollo!" Crispy blurts out.

"That lion is on his way to KAR," the receptionist says, brushing crumbs off her sweater. "This facility is closed. I'm afraid you'll have to leave."

"KAR?" I ask.

"The animal center in Knoxville. We don't have the insurance to house a lion here!" Angelica Dworfman waves her hand at us. "Now scoot. I've got to lock up."

"Knoxville Animal Research," I say under my breath. "That's bad. Very, very bad."

30
THE CHASE

"I'VE NEVER DRIVEN ON THE HIGHWAY BEFORE," Oliver says as he merges onto Highway 40.

"Can't we go any faster?" Crispy asks, his face blotchy.

"I'm going the speed limit," Oliver says. "And that's already faster than I've ever driven."

"How far ahead do you think Killjoy is?" I ask. I try not to imagine Apollo strapped down on a table with scientists experimenting on him. The bag of rocks in my stomach starts rumbling. "Poor Apollo," I whisper.

"We've got to catch up to Agent Killjoy before he hands Apollo over to KAR." Crispy has tears in his eyes.

"Don't worry. We will." I hope I'm right. My heart is

racing faster than the speed limit. *Don't freak out. Keep calm,* I tell myself. *Inhale. Exhale. Inhale. Exhale.*

When I reach out to pat Crispy's arm, I notice my hand is shaking. We can't let Killjoy sell Apollo as a guinea pig to those researchers at KAR. We just can't. I ball up my fists to keep my hands from shaking.

"At least the yellow van will be easy to spot," Butler says. "Don't worry, guys. We'll catch up to him. He's got to stop sometime to eat—"

"Or pee," Ronny interrupts.

"Keep your eyes peeled for a big yellow van," I say, straining to see out the front window.

Ronny starts giggling. "Peel your eyes."

"Like peeling the skin off a grape," Crispy adds.

I exhale loudly. "Just be on the lookout for the Animal Control van."

After an hour on the road, the sun has set and left behind a moonless night. Even a bright yellow van is going to be hard to spot in the dark. My eyes hurt from staring out the window, and my stomach is growling from missing dinner.

An orange warning light flashes on the dashboard. "We're running out of gas," Oliver says. "We'd better pull off at the next exit and get some."

"How are we going to catch Stinkerton if we get off the highway?" My question comes out as a whine.

"Sorry," Oliver says. "But if we run out of gas, we'll never catch him."

"Oh, well," I say, heartbroken. "We tried."

Oliver signals and exits the interstate at some place called Cookeville. He pulls into a gas station just off the highway and fills up the SUV. It's weird being this far away from home without Mom or Dad.

"I'm hungry," Ronny says. "Can we stop at McDonald's?" She points to the golden arches next door to the gas station.

Holy hamburger! Mom will have a cow if we eat at McDonald's. Of course, she'll have a whole herd when she finds out we went halfway to Knoxville.

"I've never eaten at McDonald's," Crispy says.

"Never?" Ronny snorts. "I'm starving."

"Okay. But let's make it fast." *Wait.* I count the money in my pocket. I only have the seven dollars and eighty-six cents I scraped together to buy the Starbucks to distract Angelica Dworfman. "Actually, we don't have enough money."

"I've never eaten at McDonald's either," Butler says. "Let's try it."

I look at my watch. It's almost five thirty. The clock is ticking and Killjoy is getting away. But what can we do? There's still a long way between us and Knoxville. And even if we see him on the highway, what then? We can't just flag him down and ask him to hand over Apollo.

Driving to Knoxville was not part of my plan. I should have thought this through before we headed into the wilds of Tennessee.

"Mom will be wondering where we are," I say to Crispy. "We probably should just give up and go home."

"Without Apollo?" Crispy's blotches go into full bloom. *Chicken-fried steak!* He's going to cry. "We'll figure it out," I say, putting my arm around his shoulders. "First, let's try those Happy Meals everyone raves about." Freddie wags his furry tail in my face. I guess he likes the idea of food.

At the drive-through window, Crispy isn't very happy when he learns Happy Meals come from dead animals. He settles on an apple pie.

I'm not hungry. The thought of giving up our search for Apollo makes me lose my appetite. Plus, I don't want to force the Patels to buy me dinner. But since they're only a dollar, I get a pie too. Ronny orders a full-on Happy Meal. Luckily, I have just enough to cover the cost.

I'm about to take a bite of my pie when I spot a familiar potbellied silhouette sitting at a picnic table in a grassy area behind the restaurant. "Wait!" I shout.

Oliver slams on the brakes, and my pie flies out of its cardboard sleeve and into the front seat.

"Killjoy. I saw him." I twist my neck to get a better look. "Drive around again. The yellow van and Apollo must be nearby."

"Unless he's on his way *back* from KAR," Ronny says with her mouth full of cheeseburger. "And already dropped off Apollo."

"Thanks for that unhappy thought," I say. Obviously, the Happy Meal isn't working.

"There!" I spot the yellow van parked across the street and nearly jump into the front seat. "Hurry, before Stinkerton comes back."

Oliver pulls in behind the van. As soon as the SUV stops, I hop out and race to the back of the van. I yank on the door, but it doesn't budge. *Red beans and rice!* It's locked. With one hand shielding my eyes, I peek through the back window. Sure enough, Apollo is curled up asleep in a corner. "He's here!" I shout.

I feel like my lungs could burst. I haven't been this happy since Santa brought me a complete spy kit when I was eight. I still have the magnifying glass and spy watch.

"Hey there!" Killjoy's booming voice is like a clap of thunder.

"He's coming!" I shout.

Agent Killjoy picks up his pace. He's practically running at me now.

My skin prickles, and my palms are sweating. I must be having a panic attack. I bang on the door to the van, but all that does is wake up Apollo, who starts howling and scratching on the other side of the door.

No! No! No! Stinkerton is closing in on me. It's no use. I can't get the door open. Afraid, I hunker alongside the van.

A shadow is approaching under the streetlights. *Aaaaak.* I almost have a heart attack. Killjoy is just a foot away from me, checking the back door of the van, his foul breath polluting the night air.

31
THE SHOWDOWN

I'VE GOT TO STOP KILLJOY AND RESCUE APOLLO. What can I use? Can I tie him up with string? Tape his hands together? I pat my pockets. *Elmer's glue!* I fumble to get it out and pull off the orange cap. I spring up from the side of the van, aim the glue at Killjoy's face, and squeeze. A glob sticks to his mustache.

I'm about to give it another squeeze when, out of the darkness, a soccer ball whizzes past me and smacks Killjoy in the jaw. The impact sends him to the ground, and he takes me with him. Stunned from the impact, I lie on the ground, wondering what's trickling into my eye. When I sit up and wipe my forehead, there's a bright red streak across my hand. *Holy hemorrhage!* I'm bleeding.

On my hands and knees, I feel for my brand-new glasses in the gravel. If I mess up my glasses again, Mom will ground me for life.

Agent Killjoy groans and then sits up, rubbing his head. He crawls over to his hat, picks it up, and places it back on his head. He stands up, glowers down at me, and then growls, "You'll never get him back."

I try to stand up, but I'm too dizzy. I must have hit my head pretty hard. I sit down again and try to focus on finding my glasses. It's tricky since it's dark and everything is blurry.

Killjoy pulls the van key from his pocket. "Where's your mother?" he growls.

I kick my foot toward his shin but miss. The effort makes me queasy.

A musky ball of fur sweeps up Killjoy's leg. The ferret stands on his hind feet on top of Killjoy's big belly, reaches out a paw, and grabs the key fob. Freddie's gone before Stinkerton knows what hit him.

"Hey, give that back, you rodent!" Killjoy yells after Freddie.

I scramble to my feet and stagger a few steps. *Whiz.* The soccer ball flies by again. It slams into the back of Stinkerton's head and knocks him to his knees. *Holy hazard!* Ronny's on a roll.

Crispy races out from the shadows and hands me the key. I'm still

dizzy and I can't see, but I have to save Apollo. I tap the key fob, stumble over to the van, open the back door, and climb inside. I open the animal cage, careful not to let Apollo escape. I push the cougar cub back inside the cage and climb in after him. I haven't come all this way to have him run away into the night.

I hear Agent Killjoy's loud curses and know I have to act fast. I slip Apollo's harness from the back pocket of my spy vest and take out the baggie of raw hamburger from another pocket. I grab a handful of mushy meat and drop it on the floor. While Apollo gobbles it down, I try to fasten the harness around his chest. He thinks it's a toy and we're playing. He's batting at the harness and grabbing it with his teeth. Every time I have it in place, he twists out of it.

"Come on, Apollo," I say. "We've got to go."

I shake the last of the hamburger from the baggie and onto the floor. Apollo goes for it. I quickly fasten the clips on the harness and then scoop him up into my arms. He squirms, making it difficult to keep my balance. Moving as fast as I can—given that I'm on my knees in the back of a van with a twenty-pound cougar cub—I scramble out of the cage and toward the open back door.

With Apollo in my arms, I'm about to climb out of the van when the door slams shut. Through the window, I make out the back of Stinkerton's sweaty shirt. He's leaning against the door.

"I'll take the lion *and* the girl to KAR if I have to!" he shouts.

I search for the door handle. *Collard greens!* The door doesn't open from the inside. Or if it does, I can't see the handle without my glasses. *Thud!* The soccer ball bounces off the van window. Killjoy ducks.

Still holding Apollo, I roll onto my back and kick at the door. Once. Twice. Three times. *Come on!* I get nowhere. It's hopeless. I can't get out. I found Apollo, but now we're both Killjoy's prisoners.

I roll over, careful not to squash Apollo, and then get to my knees again. Apollo squirms and almost slips out of my arms. I hold on to him with all my might.

I press myself against the door to get my balance. I glance out the window just in time to see Butler throw a cup of something into Stinkerton's face. No sooner has the liquid splashed into Stinky's eyes than a soccer ball hits him in the head again. *Yes!* The timing is like a well-choreographed ballet. Holding his head, Killjoy stumbles off to the side of the road.

"Get me out of here!" I shout.

Butler swings the van door open and holds his hand out. I scoot forward and take it. I'm clinging to Apollo with one hand, and Butler is trying to pull me out by the other.

"Hurry," he says.

My bottom is at the edge of the opening, but my feet don't quite reach the ground. And everything is blurry without my glasses. I stretch my legs and feel the gravel under my shoes. Apollo is struggling again. I hug him with both arms so he doesn't escape. I squeeze him as hard as I can and hop down from the van. Butler steadies me as I stand up.

I hear Agent Killjoy growling from the side of the road. Apollo growls back.

"Let's go!" Butler shouts and takes off running toward the car.

Arms straight out like Frankenstein's monster, Killjoy reaches for me with both hands. I tuck Apollo under one arm and squeeze him against my body, then pull a stale granola bar from my pocket and fling it at Killjoy. It hits him in the ear, but he keeps coming. I launch another. This time, the sharp corner of the wrapper hits him in the eye, and he stops for a second and rubs his eye. I reach into my pocket and grab my notebook and hurl it at him. It smacks him square in the face. He stops again, this time just long enough for me to get past him.

"Come on!" Butler yells. He's waiting for me with the car door open.

Oliver revs the engine. Crispy and Ronny jump into the back seat.

Holding Apollo tightly, I sprint to the SUV and climb into the back seat.

Butler shuts my door and then hops into the front. He pushes the button to lock all the doors.

"Drive!" I shout.

Oliver fastens his seat belt, glances around, signals, and then pulls out onto the road.

"Wait!" Crispy shouts. "Where's Freddie?"

"Look!" I point at Killjoy, who's mopping his face with a hanky. Right above Killjoy, crouched on top of the Animal Control van, Freddie is ready to pounce.

The ferret reaches out a paw, grabs Agent Killjoy's hat, and runs into the woods.

"Why, you rodent!" Killjoy yells and chases after him.

Like a flash, Crispy is out of the car and into the woods.

"Percy!" I shout after him. *Shiitake mushroom!* My little brother is running through a dark forest in Nowheresville, Tennessee. "Percy! Freddie!" I yell. "We've got to get home!" I know they can't hear me from inside the car. But now that I've got Apollo, there's no way I'm letting him go.

I glance at my spy watch. It's almost six thirty. At this rate, who knows when we'll get home. Mom will be having an elephant by now, and I'll be grounded for life. At least I got Apollo back. I hug him, and he licks my face. I squeeze him tighter. "I love you," I whisper into his furry ear.

"Who's that?" Ronny asks with fear in her voice. She's pointing out the window toward the trees.

I hear a thud and look out the window. Agent Stinkerton's hat is looming just outside. I gasp. Killjoy is back. Shaking, I pound my hand into the door lock. A furry tail wags in front of the window, and I get a familiar whiff of musk. "Freddie!"

I unlock the door, and Crispy—with Freddie wrapped around his neck—slides in next to me. Butler locks the doors again.

"Step on it!" I shout.

"Got him!" Crispy sounds triumphant. He's wearing Stinkerton's hat, and Freddie is chewing on its brim.

"Can we go home now?" Ronny whines. "I'm tired."

Butler reaches over the front seat and hands a round tin to Ronny. "I saved you a piece of cake. Too bad I had to use the chai on Mr. Animal Control." He smiles. "My mom always says 'nothing like cake and tea to revive the spirit.'"

Nothing like rescuing your cougar cub from the evil clutches of Animal Control after a heart-pounding life-and-death struggle to revive the spirit. The adrenaline coursing through my veins will keep me awake for the trip home.

An hour and a half later, we finally arrive back home. *Shiitake mushroom!* There's a police car in our driveway. Either

Mom called the cops or Agent Killjoy is having us arrested for stealing Apollo and leaving him stranded without the key to his van.

Yup. I still have his key fob in one of my pockets. But I did leave him with two granola bars and my favorite notebook.

Mom has tears in her eyes when she runs out to meet us. I'm barely out of the SUV when she flings her arms around me. After the hug and more tears, a torrent of angry questions rains down on me.

In response, I pull the sleeping cougar cub from the back of the car and hold him out as a peace offering.

32
THE AWARD CEREMONY

A LOT HAS HAPPENED IN THE TWO WEEKS since we brought Apollo home. I'm grounded for another month, except to go to school and to work after school at Patel's Pastries. I'm working to pay off Animal Control for the cost of sending someone out to fetch Agent Killjoy and his van.

Mom says I'll learn a valuable lesson by working to pay the fee. She's right. Mrs. Patel is teaching me how to make *kaju barfi. Yummy!* I also learned that *barf* means snow in Hindi.

Crispy's working at the bakery too. He confessed to taking stuff from Dad's town house. He'd been doing it for months. He's grounded too, except for when he's helping out at the bakery so he can buy Ronny new shin guards—Chewbacca the chimp chewed up the one he stole. And he has to visit the school counselor once a week to talk about his feelings about Mom and Dad's separation. I still think he has a crush on Ronny, but maybe he's just a klepto. Who knows?

At the injunction hearing yesterday, Dad did his lawyerly thing to prove to the county judge everything is in order at Lemontree Petting Zoo. Dad was awesome! You should have seen Agent Killjoy in the courtroom. He was fuming mad. Mom says he's jealous of Dad because Dad always wins.

Turns out, Agent Killjoy wasn't taking Apollo to an animal *research* lab; he was taking him to an animal *rescue* in Knoxville. Mom says we would have gotten Apollo back after the hearing anyway. She says Agent Killjoy was just doing his job.

Right. And I'm a polka-dotted kangaroo.

I was hoping Dad would take Mom out to lunch or something after the hearing. But I guess a courtroom isn't the most romantic setting. Hopefully, the award ceremony this afternoon will bring them back together and we can all go to Patel's Pastries afterward to celebrate. Fingers crossed.

That's right. My story about rescuing Apollo made the front page of the *Cub Reporter,* and Mrs. Cheever nominated it for the Thompson Award for Journalism. I may be a dreamer, but it's pretty cool when your dream comes true.

I check my spy watch. It's two thirty. The ceremony is at four this afternoon. I'm so excited, my chest is buzzing like the wings of a ruby-throated hummingbird.

Wait, I haven't told you the most important news. Crispy and I are setting up a pet detective agency in a storage closet in the back of Mrs. Patel's bakery. When we run out of work at the bakery, Mrs. P. lets us organize our office in the storage closet.

People are always posting notices at Mom's veterinarian clinic about lost pets, so I figure middle Tennessee could use a good pet detective. Maybe I'll put an ad in the school newspaper.

Speaking of the newspaper, Mom insists I leave my spy vest at home during the award ceremony. But you never know when you might need string or scissors or a retractable pointer. Yeah, Dad gave me another one of his old pointers to replace the one still stuck in the roof of that bat-infested shed. Even if I can't wear it, you can bet I'll have my vest with me.

For the ceremony, I am wearing my nicest blue flower-print dress to complement my auburn hair, along with black tights and my favorite boots. Mom had to replace the buckle on one of them after my escapade in the shed.

To celebrate my nomination, Mom gave me a new notebook and a cool fedora hat like the kind gangsters wear in old movies. She says all the great detectives wear hats. I slide it on my head in front of the bathroom mirror. Something's not quite right—I mean, besides my old glasses squeezing my head because they're too small. I have to wear my old ones until my new ones are ready. I tilt the hat slightly so it shades my right eye. There! Perfect.

"Petunia, you look fabulous," Mom says when she sees me coming down the stairs.

I take the stairs two at a time and then twirl around at the bottom. "That hat suits you." Mom straightens it. "Did you finish your chores already?"

Brussels sprouts! In my excitement, I forgot to do my chores. I shake my head. Now I'll have to go to the award ceremony with camel snot on my dress.

"You deserve a day off," Mom says and kisses me on the cheek.

Holy haberdashery! I should dress up more often if it gets me out of my afternoon chores.

At the award ceremony, we all sit together in the front of the gymnasium in the section reserved for nominees and their families. Mom and Dad smile at each other, but I can sense the tension. Mari talks a mile a minute to fill the void. Now I know why Ronny's such a chatterbox. *Like mother, like daughter.*

Mrs. Cheever takes the stage to announce the prizewinners. My heart is galloping, and my face is on fire. She starts with the runner-up. My palms are sweating, and I'm so nervous I could explode.

"And third place goes to K—"

I gasp.

"Kelly Finkelman." Applause drowns out my noisy exhale.

Mrs. Cheever holds up an envelope. "I'm especially proud of our next winner because this is her first full-length story for the newspaper. She's going to make an excellent reporter. Second place goes to Kassandra O'Roarke."

My mouth falls open. Crispy pokes me in the shoulder. "Go get your trophy." Mom and Dad glance at each other and smile for real. I practically trip over my own feet trying to get to the stage.

Mrs. Cheever shakes my hand and holds out a globe on a gold base with my name engraved on it. "I'd like to read the ending of Kassandra's fine article," she says, smiling at me.

Holy herald! I didn't see this coming. The wings in my chest beat against the bag of rocks in my stomach. I don't know if I should be proud or embarrassed.

Mrs. Cheever reads from my article: "*Writing about rescuing our cougar cub, I realized the true heart of my story was not kidnapping, chasing bad guys, or jailbreaks, but the generosity of my little brother, Perseus 'Crispy' O'Roarke. Crispy puts the* fun *in* malfunction." The audience laughs. "*And he taught me it's not what we have but what we share that matters.*" Mrs. Cheever looks up and winks at me.

I take my trophy and try not to fall off the stage. As I'm skipping back down the stairs toward my seat, everyone claps. Even Smelly Kelly waves at me and gives me a thumbs-up. I guess she's not so bad for a cheerleader. Mom and Dad beam at me as I take my seat. My cheeks are hot, but my heart is soaring. Crispy gives me a high five. Good thing Mrs. Cheever didn't read the rest of my article out loud or it might go to Crispy's head.

"The first-place Thompson Award goes to a promising young journalist," says Mrs. Cheever. "Butler Patel."

Butler! I didn't even know he wrote for the newspaper. I scan the audience and see Mrs. Patel standing near the back, clapping like mad.

Butler looks nice in his navy-blue suit and slicked-back hair. When he smiles at me, a weird tickling in my stomach makes me wonder if I'm hungry or getting sick or something.

Mrs. Cheever hands him a globe trophy bigger than mine. "The title of Butler's winning article is HOME. And the opening line reads, 'A house is made of wood and beams, but a home is made of love and dreams. This is the story of my family's migration to Tennessee, along with the importance of good friends and learning to see things from a different perspective.'"

Butler waves at me from the stage, and I wave back. I get that weird tickling in my stomach again. I put both hands on my tummy to tell it to hush.

"Butler's story will be published in this week's issue of the *Cub Reporter*." Mrs. Cheever claps, and the audience joins her. I hoot, and Crispy hollers, "Way to go, Butler!"

After the ceremony, Mrs. Patel invites us all back to the bakery to celebrate. It's just like I planned. We'll all be together again.

"I've got to get back to Nashville," Dad says. "Thanks anyway."

My heart sinks. My eyes are itchy, and I dig my nails into my palms.

Dad turns to me. I stare at my boots.

"I'm so proud of you." He puts his arms around me. When I hug him back, I can't help it, I start crying like a baby.

He strokes my hair. "Don't cry, sweetie. I'll see you next weekend."

Holy humidity! I can't stop sobbing. It's like I've sprung a leak.

Dad kisses the top of my head and whispers into my ear, "I love you, kiddo. I'll always be your dad no matter what."

Now, I'm bawling my head off.

Mari hands me a tissue and then moves in for a group hug. "Congratulations, *mijita*. We're all so proud of you."

Ronny puts one scrawny arm around my waist. "I don't want to go home," Ronny says, her soccer ball under her other arm. "Can I stay with Kassy?"

At that moment, I realize from a different perspective, I'm not losing a dad . . . I'm gaining a wicked soccer ball–wielding sister. I'm laughing and crying at the same time. Emotions are so confusing.

Still wiping my eyes and sniffling, I wave goodbye as Dad, Mari, and Ronny leave the gym.

Mom puts her arms around me. "You know it's not your fault your father left, right? It's nobody's fault." She squeezes me closer. "Life is sweet, even more so because of you, my sweet Petunia."

She takes my hand, and I take Crispy's. Freddie bouncing on his shoulder, Crispy skips to keep up with me and Mom. I squeeze his hand, and he smiles up at me. I swear Freddie's smiling too. As the three Mousekeeters—well, four if you count Flatulent Freddie—head to the Jeep, birds sing a sweet song as they perch on branches exploding with pink blossoms. The fragrant spring air is buzzing with life.

Later, back at the bakery, I finally get to try a piece of Mrs. Patel's coconut cake. She's decorated it with black-and-white icing, like newsprint. I'm on my second piece when the phone rings.

"Patel's Pastries," I answer the phone. When I'm working here after school, Mrs. P. always lets me answer the phone.

"Kassy?" a familiar voice asks. "You've got to help." Ronny is on the verge of tears. "Yara's gone. She's been dognapped!"

"Did you check under the beds?"

"Yes."

"Did you look in the closets?"

"Yes."

"Did you check the dryer?"

"We looked everywhere. She's gone." Ronny starts to sob. "And that's not all—" She breaks down crying. *Shih tzu puppy!* She's really upset.

After my experience with Apollo, I know just how she feels.

"Don't worry, little sis," I say as I pull my new notebook from the pocket of my spy vest. "Kassy O'Roarke, pet detective, is on the case."

ACKNOWLEDGEMENTS

THANKS TO LISA WALSH for her untiring support and encouragement, even when editing first rough drafts. Thanks to Barb Goffman for her superhero editing. And thanks to everyone at Beaver's Pond Press, especially Hanna, for seeing the book through production. Thanks to Natasha Trigo for her insightful feedback. As always, thanks to Beni for reading and egging me on. And thanks to my furry friends, Mischief and Mayhem, for keeping me company.

ABOUT THE AUTHOR

ALONG WITH *KASSY O'ROARKE: CUB REPORTER* and the other books in the Pet Detective Mysteries series, Kelly Oliver is the award-winning, best-selling author of the adult fiction Jessica James Mystery series, including *Wolf*, *Coyote*, *Fox*, *Jackal*, and *Viper*. Her debut novel, *Wolf: A Jessica James Mystery*, won the Independent Publisher's Gold Medal for Best Thriller/Mystery, was a finalist for the Foreword Magazine Award for Best Mystery, and was voted number one in Women's Mysteries on Goodreads. *Coyote* won a Silver Falchion Award for Best Mystery. *Fox* was a finalist for both the Claymore and the Silver Falchion Award, and a finalist for the Mystery and Mayhem Awards. *Jackal* is a finalist for a Silver Falchion Award.

Kelly is also the author of the historical mystery, *Miss Lemon's Mysterious Assignment at Styles*, the first in a new series.

When she's not writing novels, Kelly is a distinguished professor of philosophy at Vanderbilt University, and the author of fifteen nonfiction books and over one hundred articles on issues such as the refugee crisis, women and the media, animals, and the environment. Her latest nonfiction book, *Hunting Girls*, won a Choice Magazine Award for Outstanding Title. Her work has been published in *The New York Times* and *The Los Angeles Review of Books*, and she has been featured on ABC news, CSPAN Books and Books, the Canadian Broadcasting Network, and various radio programs. To learn more about Kelly and her books, visit www.kellyoliverbooks.com with a parent or guardian.

If you liked Kassy O'Roarke, Cub Reporter ask your parents to leave a review of the book. Reviews help Kassy and her friends keep going on adventures!